If Blake was̄ then she was.

The implication stomach. Blake knew very well that he had no right to Cranford Hall. But by marrying her he'd become the husband of the true heir.

Surely, she thought, he hadn't been covering his back by proposing to her? But it all made a horrible kind of sense.

He couldn't have faked that raw hunger. Nor the love in his eyes, surely? Was it a coincidence that they'd fallen in love? Or…had it been a calculated act to secure the inheritance for ever?

Childhood in Portsmouth meant grubby knees, flying pigtails and happiness for **Sara Wood**. Poverty drove her from typist and seaside landlady to teacher, till writing finally gave her the freedom her Romany blood craved. Happily married, she has two handsome sons: Richard is married, calm, dependable, drives tankers; Simon is a roamer—silversmith, roofer, welder, always with beautiful girls. Sara lives in the Cornish country-side. Her glamorous writing life alternates with her passion for gardening, which allows her to be carefree and grubby again!

Recent titles by the same author:

THE ITALIAN'S DEMAND
HUSBAND BY ARRANGEMENT
IN THE BILLIONAIRE'S BED

A
CONVENIENT WIFE

BY
SARA WOOD

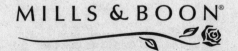

MILLS & BOON®

First published in Great Britain 2003
Harlequin Mills & Boon Limited,
Eton House, 18-24 Paradise Road, Richmond, Surrey TW9 1SR

© Sara Wood 2003

ISBN 0 263 83344 5

Set in Times Roman 10½ on 12 pt.
01-1203-50394

Printed and bound in Spain
by Litografía Rosés, S.A., Barcelona

CHAPTER ONE

THE shock silenced him. In the dimly lit room he heard nothing but his thundering heartbeat. And the voices in his head saying, it isn't true. *Can't* be!

Blake fought the red mist that clouded his brain. Generations of his ancestors must have been born, slept and finally died in the opulent surroundings of this vast bedroom. Yet he doubted that any of them had ever heard such a devastating outburst as this.

You are not the legitimate heir. You are…my love-child.

His mother's words spun around his head, destroying his ability to reason. It took a supreme effort of will for him to recover his senses. Seconds more before he realised there was a logical explanation. Her mind must be confused from the intensive course of medication.

Deeply distressed for her and with his concern for her uppermost in his thoughts, he masked his own chaotic feelings and sought to calm her. 'I've tired you with our chatting, Mother. I think you should sleep,' he advised gently.

Kay Bellamie's eyes blazed with anger, the only living sign in the once-beautiful face that was now a putty-coloured mask of imminent death.

'Don't treat me as if I'm mad!' she croaked. 'I'm perfectly sane. You are *not* a Bellamie! I want you to know that!'

'Mother!' Blake winced at her insistence, and at the destruction of her lyrical, fluting voice.

'It's the truth! You have *no right* to the inheritance. Look at yourself!' she flared. 'Do you think you have Bellamie blood? Where is your blond hair? Your fat gut? Your bulbous nose? I *know* who fathered you. It was my lover, I tell you!'

He couldn't bring himself to humour her. This was too painful and must be stopped. 'Take it easy,' he cautioned. 'Perhaps you've been dreaming—'

'No!' Her skeletal hand clutched at his, its bony fingers a series of white claws against his healthily tanned skin. 'Do you know why I refused to allow you to be called after a Bellamie ancestor? I broke with tradition because I was desperate to keep something of your father. A name that linked you with him—'

'*Blake?*' He frowned, his inky brows two uncomprehending angles.

His mother looked at him as if she saw someone else and he felt fear clutch at his stomach with a scouring ferocity. No, he thought in silent horror. Don't let it be true!

'No, I daren't use his name. Blake means dark.' For a brief moment her eyes closed and he felt a pang to see the blue pallor of her lids. 'You've seen your baby photos,' she grated. 'You know you were born with masses of raven hair. Like my lover's.' A far-away smile lifted her thin lips for a moment. 'Dear God, Blake!' she went on vehemently. 'I know this is hard but, for your own sake, accept what I'm telling you! My mind is crystal clear. I've carried this secret all your life and I *must* unburden myself before I die. For the last time, you are not the son of Darcy Bellamie!'

Exhausted, she let her hand fall away to lie limply at her side. Slowly, reluctantly, his gaze flickered in the direction of the oil painting of his father over the baroque mantelpiece. A chill settled deep within his spine and spread to his entire body till he felt as if he'd been carved from ice. How many people had commented on the total lack of resemblance?

Every ounce of his strength seemed to leave him. Once

again, rational thought had become suspended. Utterly motionless, he sat like a zombie beside her rumpled bed, feeling as if he'd been poleaxed.

What was she saying? Why? his brain screamed. But he held back his raging emotion, crushing it remorselessly as he'd been instructed every day of his childhood until he had become adept at hiding his tempestuous feelings.

Frustration gripped him. It was impossible to know why she was exerting all her meagre energy to make such an astonishing claim.

Unless it was true.

Shuddering, he sought denial because acceptance would destroy him. Tenderly he stroked her hot forehead.

'Mother. The drugs you've been prescribed are powerful sedatives and they—'

'I haven't taken any for days. I needed to think. I'm speaking the truth, I swear on my grandson's head,' she cried in desperation.

That rocked him. He sucked in a long breath to fill his crumpled lungs. Defiantly his fists clenched. Preposterous—surely? All his life he had been groomed and trained and guided by his parents, governesses, fencing masters, riding instructors and stewards in preparation for his future as the Bellamie heir.

He'd been twenty when his elderly father, Darcy, had died. From that day he'd been catapulted into a position of authority where his decisions affected the lives of many. Consequently, he had made them with great care. After eight years of such unnerving responsibility he had become supremely confident in the role which would be his until he died and his son took over.

Confident…yes. And yet, admittedly, sometimes he felt restless and increasingly resentful of the constant pressures of duty. Occasionally he just longed to be free.

The hairs rose on the back of his neck. Had he inherited

that restlessness from his true father? The stolid and conventional Bellamie men had reputedly always been content with their lot of wealth and privilege. Maybe there *wasn't* a drop of their blood in him!

But of one thing he was certain. He loved every inch of Cranford Hall, every blade of grass on the vast estate— even the handful of estate workers' cottages spilling into the adjoining village of Great Aston.

And now his mother claimed that none of this belonged to him, after all! If this was true she'd just ripped apart the very fabric of his life.

God. He couldn't handle that. He'd spent twenty-eight years living a lie. Pretending to be someone else. When he was just his mother's by-blow. Base born. Illegitimate. *A bastard!*

A sudden pain made his stomach muscles tighten. He looked at his mother, who loved him, and saw the truth written there in her pleading eyes. She was perfectly lucid, her gaze steady and focused as she fumbled with the gold locket around her neck and opened it.

He swallowed. A photograph. Fearing what he'd see, nevertheless he leant forward to peer at the miniature heart-shaped snapshot.

A young man. Dark-skinned, vital and bursting with life, with black hair that curled defiantly, exactly like his, and laughing black eyes—the mirror of his. Same bone structure. Same fire. Two peas in a pod.

'Your father,' she whispered and lovingly stroked the photograph with a shaky finger.

'No!' But he could see it was. And his heart seemed to stop with shock.

'Look at him,' she said tenderly. 'You and he are so alike.' She sighed. 'He possessed me, body and soul. I almost abandoned everything for him. But he had nothing—and I'd known poverty only too well. I wanted this for you!' she cried, flinging out a quivering arm to encompass the room and its priceless contents.

Hardly breathing at all, he sank heavily back into the chair. It was as if he'd been cast adrift on the open sea. *His father.* A whirlwind of emotions rampaged through him: anger, despair and finally a hunger for this unknown father's love, which brought a lump to his throat and the pricking of tears to his haunted eyes.

A limp blue-veined hand lifted from the raw silk coverlet and covered his. 'Blake, you know I love you,' she said with a heartbreaking tenderness. 'I've devoted my life to you. I vowed that the son of my lover must one day inherit Cranford—'

'Inherit? How? You've made my position here impossible!' he cried more harshly than he'd meant.

But he was fighting a maelstrom that seethed inside him and the words had stubbornly stuck in his throat. He didn't want to do the honourable thing and give up Cranford because he wanted to forget this conversation had ever happened. To deny that dark-eyed laughing man. To remain what he was—Blake Bellamie, master of all he surveyed, proud of his heritage.

'Why?' she whimpered.

Impatiently he began to stride about the room, trying to resist the wicked urge to remain silent and to keep his mother's secret. He and his son and Cranford were inextricably linked. They had been his whole life, his entire reason for existing.

Yet the truth hammered at him relentlessly. Searing anguish shredded his guts. Shock and fear of the future weakened the muscles of his legs, turning them to mush. He'd never known such violent feelings.

Staggering a little, he leant heavily against a chinoiserie chest making the Satsuma vases on its racks rattle alarmingly. Sick to the stomach, he knew what he must do. God, he was shaking from that decision! Never in his entire gold-plated life had he felt so ill, so diminished. So…empty and alone.

Bleak-faced, he allowed his hooded black eyes to rest moodily on his panic-stricken mother, a pathetic figure almost devoured by the huge Jacobean four-poster.

Which wasn't his. *Nothing* was his. Nothing that he'd imagined he'd inherited. Only that morning he'd ridden across *his* land, spoken to *his* tenants, walked into the pub and discussed renovations with *his* builder and carpenter over a pint of local ale. Now everything belonged to someone else. His whole life had been a sham.

And destitute, it seemed, he and his six-year-old son. Throwing his head back, he inwardly groaned. What would he tell Josef? His child, his beloved son, light of his life since his wife had left…

He covered his face with his hands and groaned. But he couldn't hide from the truth. He had to start anew. And find the man who'd sired him.

'My…real father. Where is he?' he said jerkily, appalled by his need.

'Gone. Vanished into thin air.' Tears sprang from his mother's pale eyes. 'I told him to go, said that I didn't love him even though I would have laid down my life for him, I loved him so much. Still do…'

In deep shock, he stared at the desolation expressed in her face. Never had he known his mother so fervent. Within that cool, emotionless exterior there had been a passionate woman who had sacrificed everything for him. Including her own happiness

And, rattled by his own emotional reaction, he was beginning to understand. All his life she'd drummed it into his head that showing passion was unseemly for a gentleman.

Every excessive display of his had been relentlessly

crushed until he'd realised that his innocent, natural responses of joy and sorrow and anger weren't acceptable. Whenever he'd lost his temper or had become over-exuberant he'd been punished severely.

A bitter anger swept through him. Because she'd wanted him to behave like a Bellamie he'd been denied his own personality!

There had been times when he'd felt like exploding from suppressed fire and energy within him but had been forced to control himself. That was when he rode till the wind tore at him, the speed and ferocity of his riding easing the heat from his body.

So he had inherited passion and a lust for life. What else? The restlessness, the urge to feel the wind on his face, his hatred of being cooped up indoors for hours on end?

Bitterly, he realised that it didn't matter. He must leave Cranford and start a new life. It was the right thing to do. He blanched at the burden she had placed on him and suddenly knew the name of his father.

'He was called Josef, wasn't he?' he shot and at her soft smile of acknowledgement he felt his chest tighten.

The same name as his own son. Chosen by his mother who'd claimed it had been the name of her Hungarian grandfather.

Feeling light-headed, he realised he'd been holding his breath. Letting it out in a despairing exhalation, he clung to the remnants of his self-respect. Dying inside, every word an effort, he said tightly, 'I have to find the true heir. The legitimate descendant—'

'*No*! Not Giles. Not your father's cousin!' she wailed.

'If he's the rightful heir then I am duty bound to find him,' he vowed, tearing the words out of his body one by one because they didn't want to emerge at all.

She bit her lip then, looking desperate, she blurted out

wildly, 'And inflict hell on everyone here? Giles is…' She gulped, her voice wavering. 'He's…evil, Blake!' It seemed she was struggling for words to convince him, to change the doubting frown on his face. 'Giles was a drunk! You can't turn Cranford over to him!' she sobbed. 'You have your own son to think of now!' Her hands raked at him in desperation. 'I beg you, my darling! Don't let me die knowing that my whole life, my sacrifice, has been in vain!'

His heart twisted, loving her so much that it hurt him deeply to see her distress. He listened to her hesitant and stumbling description of Giles's habits. And was sickened by the man's degrading behaviour.

Stroking his mother's deeply lined forehead, he managed to soothe her. Gave her a pill. Waited till she slept. Then with heavy steps, his tall, lean body bowed under an impossible weight, he crossed to the full length window, seeing everything with different eyes. A stranger's eyes.

Not his. *Not his*. He swayed, crushed by the cruel pain of knowing.

What should he do? The right thing? Or what would be best for the majority of people? Including himself. He groaned. How could he be objective about this?

Josef appeared. Solemnly sitting on his new pony, chatting happily to Susie, the groom. Love swelled in his heart. And, when Blake swept his dark and troubled gaze over the parkland and wooded hills beyond, he felt a visceral tug of belonging that could never be expunged from his system.

Giles was an evil man. The estate, the business, the tenants—all would suffer in his hands. Blake knew this was no longer a decision based on his own desires but the cold, hard fact that Giles would go through the Bellamie millions like a knife through butter.

He had no choice. For the sake of everyone who depended on him he would keep the secret.

Even so, his life would never be the same. Already he felt a fraud. Shadows had already begun to darken his life, to weigh down his heart. He wondered with a bleak fury if he could ever be truly happy again.

CHAPTER TWO

'I SUPPOSE you're wondering why I've invited you to a meal just three weeks after my father's death.'

Despite the almost defiant set of her chic blonde head Nicole Vaseux was aware that the tremor in her voice had betrayed how she really felt. Forcing a feeble cover-up smile, she studied her guests who were seated around the long table beneath a rampaging grape vine. There was sympathy in her friends' faces for the death of her father, Giles, and they were making small, encouraging noises for her to continue.

Reaching out with her long fingers, she fiddled nervously with her cutlery making the silver bangles on her wrist jangle noisily. Almost certainly her friends would try to stop her leaving the country, thinking she was in no fit state to transport herself and a seven-week-old baby to England. They'd be right, of course.

Her mouth, as crimson and as lavish as her flowing dress, became tight with tension. After the blows that life had dealt her lately she felt as if she'd been hit by a pile-driver and all but driven into the ground.

'It's a kind of temporary goodbye,' she ventured, as casually as possible.

There was a sudden silence, knives and forks being suspended in mid-air. They were used to her unpredictability but they obviously sensed that even she felt in two minds about her forthcoming announcement. Here goes, she thought.

'I'm driving to England tomorrow.' Her chin lifted in a show of bravado. 'I don't know how long I'll be away.'

14

Eyes widened. Mouths dropped open. Edgily she pushed away her untouched plate and braced herself for the protests. She didn't have long to wait.

'*Chérie!* It is too soon. You have a tiny baby—!'

'But he's an angel. Look how peacefully he sleeps!' she said, her husky voice low and loving. And she felt hearts soften around her.

They all looked towards the Moses basket beneath the olive tree where the fair-haired Luc slept and Nicole took advantage of their doting smiles, launching with, 'It'll be easier to go now than when he's more active.'

Adjusting the bootlace strap that had slid from her slender shoulder, she took a deep breath. For a moment she was distracted from the matter in hand when the gazes of the men in the party zoomed in like Exocet missiles on the deep ravine between her swelling breasts. There was a sudden chill emanating from the women. Startled by the unexpected sexiness of her post-baby body, she placed her arms strategically before concentrating on her bombshell.

'I must go,' she insisted. 'I have no choice. Father asked me to scatter his ashes in an English churchyard.'

'*Mon Dieu!*'

There was a buzz of chatter around the table. Their surprise almost equalled hers—and she'd been stunned by the request.

'But Nicole, you were born in the Dordogne!'

'With dual nationality—'

'And an English *mother*—'

'Surely your father was French—Giles Bellamie... A French name, yes? And you, so chic, so...artistic...'

'I know.' She sighed, the unconsciously elegant shrug of her shoulders expressing her utter mystification. 'But he was actually born in a village called Great Aston. In the Cotswolds.' She stumbled a little over the unfamiliar name.

Voices clamoured. She barely heard them. Her head ached with the thinking she'd done recently, with the trauma of her divorce, the birth of her child, the death of her father. Too much for anyone to bear, even a fatalist like herself. And now this, out of the blue.

Her father had been utterly French in style and outlook, though they'd always spoken English in the house. Even her mother—long divorced from her father and now living in New York with her new husband—knew nothing of the British passport tucked in the back of the locked desk drawer.

In a state of shock, Nicole had found the village on a map. It lay in an area called the Cotswolds, a rural part of England.

She had recognised the name of Stratford-upon-Avon which was to the north since that was Shakespeare country, and the city of Bath to the south-west. Close to Great Aston was Broadway, the mecca for tourists seeking a quaint, historical English village.

It must be lovely there, she'd thought. And had felt less resentful of the need to make the trip.

'It's an interesting area. I thought I'd make it a holiday,' she announced into the babble of English and French. 'I need one, badly.' She rolled her eyes, making fun of her troubles, and took a sip of her mineral water.

'I'll take you,' announced Louis.

'No, I will. I know England!' insisted Leon.

Nicole had noticed how their eyes had darkened speculatively as their gazes had strayed yet again to the honeyed mounds above the silk slip dress which hugged her newly curvaceous body. She sighed. Men! The last thing she needed was a sexual interlude right now. Her libido was non-existent. She had other priorities now.

'Thanks, but no.' There was a noticeable relaxation amongst the women. Nicole deeply regretted the change in her friends' attitude towards her. She felt suddenly very alone, a different person now she was no longer married. And, apparently, a dangerous woman. 'I need time to grieve,' she explained. 'It will be what the Americans call "closure". And then I can play the tourist, come home and fling myself into life again.'

They nodded in agreement, several of the men reminding her to make sure she came back.

'Why would I ever want to live anywhere else?' Her graceful artist's hand indicated the million-dollar view from her father's—no, *her*—cottage. The fruit trees were laden with blossom. The scent of herbs permeated the air. Bees darted busily among the unusual flowers her father had planted.

She went pale and the deep blue of her eyes took on a grey hue as a chill slid like cubes of ice down her spine. This was an English style garden. Like the many English ex-pats in the Dordogne he'd been recreating a little patch of England in a foreign country.

Forgetting her guests, she stared blankly at the tumbling roses, the lilies, the sweetly perfumed lilac. Her troubled mind resounded with the word *why*?

Why had he never told her his secret, when they'd been so close? Why had he never left France during her lifetime? Had he hated his birthplace—or was there another darker reason why he'd turned his back on his country?

Despite the warm evening she shivered. It was a secret she must unravel. However long it took.

'There's a lady chucking dust about in the graveyard! And she's got a hunchback on her tummy!'

An unusually excited Josef came hurtling into the church and down the nave as if he'd been shot from a gun. Still in his Sunday best—though decidedly grubbier than when he'd set out for church an hour earlier—the sparkling-eyed Josef skidded to a halt in front of his sombre-faced father who was indulging in a convivial after-service coffee in the nave.

Almost two weeks had passed since Blake had learnt he had no right to control Cranford. But he'd promised his mother that he wouldn't act hastily. His days and nights had been filled with questions, his conscience had crucified him every time he'd taken a decision concerning the estate.

Only Josef had given him heart. He smiled at his son, reflecting that he was well used to Josef's novel way with words. There'd be a rational explanation—there always was. A woman in her late pregnancy, perhaps. Though, he mused ruefully, Josef knew all about pregnant women and could identify them with ear-piercing certainty.

Politely excusing himself, Blake put down his coffee cup to deal with his son's latest misunderstanding, conscious that everyone there was indulgently watching his much-adored son whose joyous attack on life caused more smiles than offence.

'Why do you think she's doing that?' he asked, unable to stop himself from curving his palm lovingly around Josef's eager face. In a flash he knew why his mother had sacrificed so much for *him*. Of course you did. Your children held your sanity, your heart and brain in their tiny hands. You would go through hell for them. Sacrifice whatever you must to ensure their survival. It was a biological drive that ensured you defended your child, the future of the human race, against all harm.

''Cos she's mad,' Josef declared. 'She's talking rubbish to herself, like she's saying spells. And crying.'

'Crying?' Blake frowned and exchanged a concerned glance with the Reverend Thomas. 'Paul, I think I'd better see what I can do to help.'

Reaching for his son's hand he loped off, his long legs

covering the ground so quickly that Josef was obliged
to trot.

No one questioned his authority. The small group clus-
tered together for refreshments after Sunday worship had
always deferred to the Bellamies. As had their ancestors,
willingly and unwillingly, for more than five hundred
years—though this particular Bellamie, everyone agreed,
was an absolute gem.

Emerging from the church where countless Bellamie
forebears lay peacefully beneath stone effigies and bold
brass inscriptions, he couldn't help but catch his breath in
awe, despite the familiarity of the view. Behind the small
churchyard were the higgledy-piggledy roofs of the old
weavers' cottages, the sun turning the Cotswold stone slabs
to gold. Glorious parkland spread out in the valley beyond
them, green and lush and merging with the petticoat of
woods at the foot of Cranford Hill.

Blake knew that he owed this beauty, this precious heritage, to the fact that for hundreds of years the Cotswolds
had produced the finest wool in Europe. He beamed with
pride.

The Sunday silence was sweetly pierced by the sound
of birdsong and the gentle hum of honey bees. He felt a
pang of unutterable love. This place had become a part of
him—body, soul, heart, mind. It was his and he was it.
Legitimate or not, he was its temporary warden, dedicated
to its welfare and its preservation until his son inherited—

'She's gone, Daddy! Has she magicked herself invillible?'

'Invisible,' he corrected automatically. 'Let's see.'

'But you can't *see* invillible!' argued his son.

He laughed. 'True! Perhaps there'll be some mystical
sign?'

Amused, he began to walk around the ancient church in

search of her with Josef crushing his hand nervously and taking exaggerated tiptoe steps. Blake's heart glowed with love and he wondered if all parents were so hugely entertained by the funny things their children did.

They saw the woman just beyond the thousand-year-old yew, its ancient branches so massive and heavy that its limbs had been supported in the eighteenth century with sturdy props.

Slim and with curves in all the right places, she was crouching on her haunches by a gravestone so he couldn't see the alleged hunchback. For a moment he caught a glimpse of her face when she looked to one side and he estimated her age as somewhere around twenty-four or five.

Her clothes were unusual—a softly flowing long skirt in what his mother would have called eau-de-nil, teamed with a figure-hugging cotton top that exposed a good two inches or more of a golden-skinned back. And yet she looked stylish. Perhaps it was the trailing silk scarf, elegantly draped around her long neck.

Her pale blonde hair had been expensively cut, the silken strands swinging gently forward in a glistening arc as her slender and tapering fingers moved slowly over the lichen-covered stone. Not your average madwoman, he thought, intrigued by her sophistication, her chic.

'She's *feelin'* the grave!' his son whispered. 'Bet she's blind, too!'

Worrying about Josef's startling ability to put both feet in his mouth, Blake adopted a stern expression.

'Hush. Don't say a *word*. Understand? Leave this to me.'

He watched Josef's mouth adopt a comical zipped-up shape and suppressed a faint smile. How he loved his eager, caring son! He was doing the right thing in retaining the inheritance. He felt sure. And crushed the little voice within his innermost soul which disagreed.

They walked towards her, the warm April sunshine caressing his back and the scent of lilac from the rectory garden pleasing his senses with its fragrance.

Blake knew that he would serve Cranford better than the evil Giles. He had earned his right to the inheritance. Even though that insistently nagging voice kept ripping through his guts by saying, *Impostor. Charlatan. Liar.*

Nicole groaned. Here was yet another indecipherable grave! She felt close to despair and wondered if she would ever find evidence of her late father's family. Still clutching the now-empty jar of his ashes, she crouched down beside the next gravestone and tried to see if it bore the name Bellamie. But that, too, was badly weathered and the fresh disappointment hit her hard.

Ever since she'd arrived in Great Aston she had felt a passionate need to find her roots in this lovely English village. Its peace and serenity had folded around her aching heart as if reaching out to comfort her.

The entire village had seemed to be drowsing in the silent Sunday morning, the stone of its picturesque cottages a pleasing honeyed shade in the warm sunshine. The palette of colours ranged through golds, greens and whites, enhanced by the soft pastels of spring flowers. The gentle hues had a soothing effect on her travel-weary mind.

It was all very English. Fallen magnolia petals littered the road from a tree which leaned over a mellow stone wall. Opposite the church drowsed a timbered pub with a quaintly thatched post office right next to it. Just beyond, she could see a small village green, complete with pond and ducks and a crumbling market cross.

On the way to the small church she'd felt the overwhelming sense that she was walking in her father's footsteps. As a child, she felt sure he must have wandered these lanes. He had been here. Skipping along, laughing with friends...

The knowledge stirred her in a way she'd never known before. It was almost a feeling of being welcomed back by loving arms after a long time away. For the first time she understood the wonderful completeness in knowing your roots, your past.

She frowned. Why her father had left such a lovely place remained a nagging mystery. Still, whatever the truth, she had done as he'd asked. Returned his ashes to the foot of the great yew tree.

And now she was on her second quest, searching for evidence of her father's relatives. But not one solitary person in this graveyard had been called Bellamie!

Depressed by her lack of success and choked by her farewell to her father, she let out a sigh. *'Papa! Quelle trahison!'* she mourned, her forehead resting against the weathered stone. What a betrayal of their closeness!

Then she stiffened. Something made her turn her head, though she'd heard no sound. Through a fine veil of tears she saw the figures of a tall dark man and a tousle-haired child a few yards away, anxiously staring at her.

Knowing how odd she must have looked, Nicole blushed and instantly scrambled to her feet, her arms cradling the weight slung around her chest.

The man's dark, sparkling eyes suddenly crinkled with laughter. Eyes so deep and glittering that she felt disorientated for a moment, as if she'd slipped into the black void of unconsciousness. But one that was warm, velvety, thrilling...

'A baby! Josef, the lady has a baby in a sling!' The man whispered to the goggle-eyed boy beside him and the child's crimped-up mouth unravelled.

'I fought it was a hunchback. Hunchtummy,' he announced, then hastily folded his lips in again.

Nicole swam back from the velvet pit and came back to reality. *'Comment?'* she cried, not realising in her confusion that she was still speaking French.

'Une bossue,' the man solemnly explained and a little giggle of surprise flew unexpectedly from her lips. A hunchback! How funny! Her soft blue gaze regarded the man who had turned to his son, gently admonishing him with, 'And it's *thought*, Josef, not "fought".' His hypnotic liquid eyes met hers again. *'Bonjour, Madame. Je m'appele Blake...'*

'Good morning, Blake!' she said hastily, impressed by his knowledge of French. She smiled. 'I do speak English. My mother came from London and we used English most of the time. I'm Nicole Vaseux,' she offered. 'And my hunchtummy is called Luc,' she informed Josef in amusement, captivated by the child's enormous black eyes. 'He's seven weeks old.'

To Nicole's surprise the little boy's tousled dark head tilted to one side and he looked deeply upset. 'Oh, dear! Did you bring him here 'cos he's dead?' he enquired unhappily.

'Josef!'

Suppressing more giggles, Nicole calmed the man's horrified gasp of protest with a pacifying shake of her head that sent her blonde hair bouncing. 'No! Look. He's fine. Just asleep.' Crouching down again in a lithe, easy movement, she let the little boy inspect her son for signs of life.

'He's breathin'!'

She nodded, enchanted by Josef's delight and relief. With her face soft and adoring, she joined him in gazing in wonder at the little scrap of flesh and blood that was her son. Huge waves of love welled up inside her and she gently kissed Luc's peachy little cheek. He was her life. His welfare would come above everything else.

'Mon chou,' she murmured.

'Is that a magic spell?' gasped Josef, backing away hastily.

Her eyes twinkled at his awe-struck face. 'Do I look like a witch?'

'You could be in disguise,' he replied cautiously.

'I'm not. This is how I am,' she said, merrily gesturing at herself. 'I was speaking French, that's all. It means my pet, my darling,' she explained and, seeing the little boy's contented grin, she stood up again, suddenly becoming aware that Blake had been watching her intently.

A *frisson* shivered through her body. He was extraordinary in every way. *Different*, though she couldn't quite decide how. He was certainly the first man ever to scramble her brains!

Tall and immaculately dressed in a soft grey suit whose quality and cut she immediately appreciated, he had opted for individuality by teaming it with a Lake Blue shirt and violet tie. With a wilting daisy in his buttonhole. She smiled, suspecting that was the child's doing.

The face above was anything but formal—tanned, outdoor and healthy, his wide mouth and strong nose and brows forming a face of immense character. The hair, too, was unconventional. Inky black like a raven's wing, it tumbled in well-groomed waves to a length far beyond that which she'd imagined any English country gentleman might favour. It gave him a raffish air which she rather liked.

The intense quality of his liquid brown eyes seemed to note everything about her. Suddenly she was conscious of her travel-creased skirt and tear-stained face. She was a mess! And, having been brought up as a Frenchwoman, she minded dreadfully.

Nicole set about bringing order to her appearance, dabbing at her eyes with a soft linen handkerchief and smoothing her hands over her hips to ease any creases.

'I'm sorry,' he said gently as she replaced her handker-chief. 'Forgive me for intruding. I thought you might be—'

'Mad,' Josef provided with great enthusiasm. Blake's glare was met with an innocent protest. 'Well, what about her chuckin'—?'

'*Throwing* would be a better choice,' his father said. 'Joe, I think you'd better see if you can help the vicar and his ladies to clear away the coffee things. There might be a chocolate biscuit left for your reward.'

'He wants me to go,' the boy explained with a 'tut' and a heavy 'adults are so transparent' sigh. Nicole wanted to laugh and for the first time in days her spirits lifted. The child took a few steps towards the church then turned. 'But you'll tell me why she chu...*threw* that dust, won't you, Daddy?'

'Go!' Blake thundered. And turned to Nicole who was having difficulty keeping a straight face. He seemed to think she was wincing because he frowned. 'I can only apologise again,' he said quietly. 'Tact isn't in his vocab-ulary, but I am persevering and thinking of tattooing the word on to his forehead. What do you think?'

She noticed how his eyes glowed with sincerity and warmth. A likeable man, one to be trusted.

'A losing battle!' she said with a little laugh.

Blake sighed. 'I think you're right. Sorry.'

'It's all right. In fact, I was very sad and he's brightened my day.'

The most beatific smile lit his face, his even teeth a dazzling white against the Caribbean tan.

'Sometimes I think it's his purpose in life,' he said fondly.

She liked him even more. He evidently adored his son and had never crushed the child's wonderful spirit. Having been brought up unconventionally, she valued that im-mensely.

'You adore him,' she murmured.

The radiance of his expression shook her. 'With all my heart,' he confessed. And he laughed. 'Is it so obvious?'

She laughed too. 'Transparent. But it's understandable.' Her hand caressed her baby's head. To her astonishment she found herself saying to this complete stranger, 'When Luc was born I learnt what it means to love someone with my whole mind, with every beat of my heart. I loved my father, but this—'

'I know,' he said softly. 'I'm besotted too. Hopeless, aren't we?'

They both laughed at their mutual captivation.

'I think I should explain my behaviour here,' she said.

'I am intrigued,' he admitted.

Her eyes grew sombre. 'I came here to spread my father's ashes on the ground. It was his dying wish.'

The smile vanished, his face softening into lines of sympathy. 'I see.'

Churned up anew after her emotional goodbyes to her father, she said croakily, 'Maybe I should have asked the vicar, but the church service was on and I didn't want to disturb anyone—'

'It's fine,' he said, the tender understanding in his voice making her eyes briefly film with tears again. 'I wouldn't have intruded but Josef dashed in to say the lady was crying outside and I was concerned.'

'Not only that—' she suggested wryly '—you were curious about the hunchtummy!'

He grinned, dazzling her with the radiance of his smile. 'Guilty!'

'I was…talking to my father. Saying a prayer and…' She broke off. The stranger didn't need to know that she had spilled her heart out, asking her father *why*?

Sadly she surveyed the wild flowers beneath the yew tree where she had scattered his ashes and felt a huge sense of loss roll through her. There was a silence but it seemed friendly and encouraging and she found herself confessing, 'I wish I didn't have to leave him here. So alone. Far from home.'

'It was what he wanted,' came the quiet and consoling reply.

'I know, but...' White and even, her teeth bit hard into her lower lip. 'I suppose I'm being selfish. Because I'll be going home soon. And he'll be here, in a foreign land...'

'Where he longed to be.' The strong and calming tones washed over her, steadying her a little. 'I can understand that this must be hard for you, though. You think you're abandoning him and his memories. But you've done what he asked and he must have had a good reason.'

Oh, Father! What reason? she agonised. Again Blake's sympathy brought the tears pricking the backs of her eyes and she struggled to overcome them. Riven with sadness she gloomily watched a yellow butterfly dancing from flower to flower. *Citron* had been her father's favourite colour. He'd always worn yellow shirts, she thought mournfully.

'I'll miss him so much. We were very close, as I was his only child,' she murmured, following the dancing butterfly as it fluttered up to the soft blue sky and disappeared.

'Then you and he were very lucky.'

'Yes, we were,' she agreed and felt comforted.

There was a moment's silence then he added with great gentleness, 'Maybe it will help a little if I tell you of an experience I had, long ago when my grandmother died. I was only seven and I found the idea of death quite terrible. It gave me nightmares. But my mother told me of an old legend—' He hesitated, looking doubtful. 'You might find this fanciful...' His voice tailed away.

Nicole was very still, her huge eyes fixed on his.

Already a sensation of calm was stealing over her. 'Go on,' she said, longing to be consoled.

Blake's face softened. 'I was reminded of the legend,' he reflected, 'when the Brimstone—the yellow butterfly— appeared just now. It's unusually early this year, which is why I noticed it. My mother told me that robins and butterflies are said to appear to people who've lost a loved one, people who are inconsolable with grief. She said it was a sign that the soul is eternal and never dies.'

She smiled. True or not, the legend had eased the weight of sorrow that had filled her heart. 'Thank you for telling me,' she said gratefully. And quivered at the warm smile he bestowed on her. 'What about you?' she asked, confused by her disturbed feelings and desperately seeking normality. 'Did the legend come true for you?'

'Not to begin with,' he replied amiably, 'though I kept looking. Then ten days later I saw a robin on grandma's favourite seat in the garden. I felt as if she'd tried to comfort me.' He frowned for a moment and continued slowly, 'Even if...' He paused and then continued. 'If I hadn't been related to her I believe she would have reached out in some way because of the love between us. I firmly believe love never dies and that a spiritual thread has continued to link us. So I believe that there will always be a thread connecting you and your father, Nicole.'

Enormously soothed by his huskily spoken words, she looked at him with deep gratitude, her lashes spiky around her huge, misted eyes. How fortunate she was to have met such a kind person at this time. Without him—and his son—the whole episode would have been traumatic.

'That's a lovely thought. I'll remember that. Thank you,' she said simply, the limpid depths of her eyes telling him more than she could say.

For a moment he stared at her as if in a trance, then snapped himself out of it with a brisk, 'Look, I don't know what you'll think of our very English coffee, but we can offer a cup of instant in the church—or you could have proper coffee, even something a little stronger, in my house if you need fortifying. You and your husband are welcome—'

'I don't have a husband at all,' she broke in, lowering her eyes to gaze at Luc's small, vulnerable head. 'I'm on my own,' she said jerkily.

The nightmare of Jean-Paul's betrayal still had the power to hurt her. How could she ever forget such pain? It had been like walking into a brick wall when, three months pregnant, she'd found Jean-Paul in bed with her supposed best friend. Nicole winced, her face wrenching with a spasm of anguish. According to him, it had been her fault. Luc had not been planned and, although she'd been thrilled, Jean-Paul had been appalled. He'd never wanted her to have a child. He'd hated her pregnancy and the way her figure had disappeared.

Stupidly, mindful of the child she carried, she'd forgiven him. And two weeks later she had returned early from work feeling horribly sick, only to discover her husband and her 'friend' in bed again.

It was then that her love for Jean-Paul Vaseux had died. Her father had warned her about love. Enjoy sex, he'd advised her. But don't mistake it for love. Love comes but rarely. And it hurts. He was right. It did. And how appropriate, she thought with a flash of waspishness, that *vaseux* meant slimy, seedy, spineless!

She noticed that Blake was looking at her baby with sadness and she felt the wave of compassion reaching out to her. And suddenly his offer was doubly welcome. She craved human company for a while, someone who was caring and who could calm her jagged nerves. The last hour had tested her reserves to the limit.

Her hand went to her brow. She felt bone-weary from

it all. Sheer physical exhaustion was taking its toll. Hours of driving, feeding Luc, missing meals and precious sleep...

'You look all in,' he said in concern. 'Please come and rest for a while, if only for your baby's sake.'

'You're very kind.' She pushed her hair back behind her ears, managing a small smile for her saviour. 'A good Samaritan. Coffee of any sort would be wonderful. I seem to have been driving for ever—'

'From France? With a baby?' he enquired, lifting a thick eyebrow in a perfectly shaped and somehow appealingly devilish V.

'I travelled over several days.'

'Heaving baby stuff in and out of your car and into hotels en route?'

Her eyes kindled. He was one of those people who found no difficulty in putting himself in other people's shoes.

'It was a nightmare,' she confessed. 'There is a bonus, though. I could lift weights for France if I ever need a new career.' She faked a weightlifter's snatch and lift then remembered she didn't have any French blood in her veins. How odd. She was English through and through. It took a bit of getting used to.

Blake was laughing, his handsome face sparkling with vitality. His amusement was so infectious that she began to grin too and her momentary pang soon passed.

'That's certainly a plus,' he conceded, chuckling. 'But it must have been tough travelling on your own.'

Her nose wrinkled. 'Not one of the best times in my life. Apart from Luc and hotel concierges, I didn't speak to a living soul the entire time.'

Though she'd felt lonely even before that. Her father's Bohemian—and sometimes raucous—friends had ceased to visit the cottage. As far as her own friends were con-

cerned, initially she'd been swamped by loving concern,
but either they were single men who looked ready to make
a move on her or they were part of a doting couple whose
affection towards one another pointed up her own failed
relationship. Gradually there had been that shift in the attitude of all her female friends now that she was divorced,
available and still potentially sexually active. It seemed
that she'd gone from being everyone's best mate to a dangerous *femme fatale*. The ripening of her body didn't help,
of course. She'd always been skinny before…

'Where have you come from?' Blake asked, interrupting
her thoughts.

An image of the cottage came to mind. Her father on
the terrace, a glass of wine in his hand, his voice slurred
with alcohol as he told her he had a short time to live.
Impatiently she roused herself from this maudlin diversion.
'I live in the Dordogne.'

'Ah. That explains it. The land of English ex-pats.'

'Except… I always thought my father was French!' she
blurted out on impulse. 'I never knew he had any English
connections till I saw his British passport,' she cried. 'He
was born here. I didn't have any idea till he…'

Her voice faltered and he stepped forward in concern,
slipping his hands beneath her elbows for support. Something peculiar happened. It started in her breast and shot
in milliseconds down to her womb. Almost as if he'd electrified the whole of her nervous system.

'Gently, gently. It's all right,' he soothed, but that
wasn't true at all.

Her emotions were going into overdrive. She wanted to
burst into tears again. And have him hold her, stroke her
into quiescence, murmur to her in that honey-gold voice
that seemed to seep into her bones and melt them. *Quelle
folie!* How vulnerable grief had made her to a kind word
and gesture!

'Excuse me,' she mumbled, pink with embarrassment. Dashing her hands across her eyes she squared her shoulders in determination. 'I'm being so stupid—'

'I don't think so. Your father. A new baby. The long journey,' he began, warming her heart with his consideration and understanding.

'Yes,' she agreed. And little did he know that there was so much more to cope with! She had to find her father's family. Suddenly her stomach grumbled in complaint and she clutched at her bare midriff, realising how hungry she was. 'As you can hear from the sound effects—' she said with an apologetic smile '—I'm in desperate need of food! I think I'd better find somewhere to eat. And he'll need feeding soon, too.' Her hand curved lovingly around baby Luc's head, enjoying its silky warmth. 'I feel odd. Woozy, as my fa-father used to say.' She managed a brave smile. 'My blood sugar level is probably non-existent,' she explained softly. 'I missed breakfast and—'

'Right. In that case, come.'

His authority was so compelling that she was being guided along the path before she knew what was happening. He strode with an ease that suggested a dangerous, feral prowl, a liquid-limbed lion lording it over the entire jungle.

And that weird fizzing sensation was attacking her again. It was like being hooked up to a pylon. Odd, how the combination of lack of food and a handsome charmer could make your head reel. She pulled away, unnerved that a stranger could be making such a dramatic impact on her. None of her male friends had made the slightest dent in her armour-clad libido.

But her defences had been weakened by events, she knew that. If she wasn't careful, she'd be flinging herself weeping into his welcoming arms and making a right fool of herself. Despite her longing for someone to cuddle her, it was time to make a run for it while her dignity was still intact!

'I don't want to take up any more of your time. I'll go to the pub,' she said, quite appalled that she felt grumpy about meeting his wife and having her romantic illusions of Blake's feral nature tainted by domesticity. 'There's one in the village. And you must be wondering where your son is—'

'In the church. Being petted and indulged. I'll tell him I'm leaving. No doubt he'll come home under escort with a stomach bulging with chocolate biscuits and his head full of misunderstandings which I'll have to unravel when he repeats them.' Blake's eyes twinkled. 'The ladies adore him. They'll probably all insist on accompanying him home so they can regale me with the funny things he's said.'

'I'm sure. All the more reason to refuse your kind offer,' she said reluctantly, liking him far too much—his ready smile, his kindness, his increasingly compelling sexiness. When had she ever met a man who was compassionate, gorgeous and not the slightest bit self-centred? And, she thought shakily, who electrified her. With difficulty, she forced herself to say a half-truth. 'I'd like to eat in the pub, anyway. It'll be fun.'

He stopped and she felt ridiculously flattered that he looked disappointed. 'As you wish. If you're sure you'll be all right on your own.'

'I have to get used to that,' she replied gravely.

'That's true. Nevertheless, I admire your strength.'

Their eyes locked and there was, indeed, admiration in his glance. It seemed to heat her through and through, coiling like a fiery cognac into her veins and quickening her pulses.

The light-headed sensation came back and she knew she had to eat before she fainted from lack of food and a surfeit of charisma. Yet she hesitated. This was, after all, a golden opportunity. A caring man, anxious to help her.

'Blake… There *is* something you can do for me before I go,' she ventured. Her heart thudded.

He looked inordinately pleased. 'Name it.'

For a moment she thought from the simmer in his eyes that he was flirting with her. Then her sense of reality returned. This was human kindness, nothing more. A man who smiled with his entire being and projected an embracing warmth without even knowing he did so.

He'd do his best to help her. Hope glowed in her eyes. She'd solve the mystery and go home content. She took a steadying breath, feeling quite excited. 'I'm trying to discover why my father wanted me to come here with his ashes,' she explained. 'You live locally, do you?'

He gave a wry smile as if thinking of a sweet-sour secret. 'I was born here. And…my parents and grandparents before me.'

Her face lit up with unconfined joy. 'Then you might be just the person I've been looking for!'

'Might I?' he murmured.

Initially, his response took her aback. Again there was that subtle shift in his expression. A deeper meaning in his eyes that made her insides turn to water. But after she'd blinked she saw that she'd been mistaken and his face showed merely a polite interest.

Oh, Nicole! she thought in reproach. How badly you need to be loved! Time she filled up with a good steak and fries. *After* she'd pumped her knight in shining armour for information.

'Yes,' she said, managing to sound brisk instead of lovelorn. 'The fact is that I've been searching the gravestones to see if any of my father's family were buried here. But they aren't, as far as I can tell. It's impossible to read many of the stones because of the…er…the…'

'Lichen,' he supplied genially, realising she was searching for the word. 'I'm afraid the frost has damaged most of the older inscriptions, too.'

He thrust his hands into his trouser pockets and smiled again. Nicole tried not to let her attraction for him show. But he was the most electrifying man she'd ever met and she wasn't very successful.

'So,' he murmured when she stood staring hazily at him. She blushed, realising that many women had probably looked at him with the same doe-eyed adoration. He'd probably dealt with them all by adopting that shuttered look. 'If you're searching for the name Vaseux,' he said, 'then I'm afraid I don't know of—'

'Oh, no!' she broke in hastily. 'My father's name wasn't Vaseux.'

'No?'

Picking up the cue, he looked at her hand and frowned because it was bare of any rings. But in her eagerness she didn't pause to explain that she'd hurled her wedding ring at Jean-Paul in fury. Tense with hope she took a deep breath, willing him to know something, anything, about her family.

'No.' She stared up at him, taut with hope. 'It was Bellamie,' she cried.

'Bellamie?'

She cringed, bewildered by his reaction. The smile had been wiped from his face and replaced by an expression of sheer alarm.

'Ye-e-es…why?'

'Bellamie!'

Nicole felt horribly sick. In a perfectly kind and courteous man, her father's surname had provoked a horrified response. Her senses reeled. Why, why? She knew with a feeling of utter dread that it was because of something awful that had happened.

She let out a small groan. If she could have taken back her request for help she would. It had been a mistake to probe into the past. She should have scattered the ashes and gone home, none the wiser. Now her father's memory was about to be sullied with some awful revelation. And she didn't want to hear it.

CHAPTER THREE

WHEN Luc began to cry she didn't know whether to be glad or sorry. His yells seared into her brain, making her incapable of coherent thought. Shaken immeasurably by Blake's reaction, she did her best to soothe her baby but his hysterical cries only grew louder and her own agitation increased till she felt like screaming herself.

It was no use. She'd have to feed him. And she needed to sit down before she collapsed anyway. Her whole body had begun to tremble with a terror of the unknown.

'Excuse me,' she squeaked in panic, searching around desperately for a convenient place to sit. She jerked out unnecessarily, 'He needs feeding.'

'There's a bench over here.' The tone was curt and laced with a steely hardness. This time the guiding hand beneath her elbow seemed to push her along without ceremony.

She could hardly collect her thoughts, they were churning so furiously in her head. He must see how shallow her breath was, how swiftly her chest rose and fell. And there were two prominent red spots of heat that she knew must stain her cheeks, together with the tenseness of her muscles which were so taut that she trembled as if she had the ague.

Thankfully she sank to the wooden seat beneath a bower of pear blossom. Such a pretty spot. Ironically, such a nightmare moment.

Not daring to look at Blake, she concentrated on extricating the yelling Luc from the sling and sliding it off, taking twice as long as usual because her fingers had become suddenly clumsy in her panic.

Father, what have you done?

In distress she bent her head, hoping Blake would go but he remained firmly planted in front of her as if on guard. Perhaps he thought she was a danger to society? she thought hysterically. It amazed her that she could feel his hostility as if it were a living thing, the power of his seething presence overwhelming her.

Quivering from the onslaught of his—as yet—unspoken disapproval, she shrank into the seat, the hard slats digging painfully into her back.

Desperately pleading with Luc to be calm, she fumbled awkwardly with the buttons of her shirt. Normally she felt no qualms about discreetly feeding her baby in public. But there was something so rawly masculine about Blake that she felt intensely aware of her body. And he wouldn't stop staring at her. Those diamond glinting eyes would examine every move she made, assess the curves of her breast... She quivered.

Luc yelled on. Modesty, she thought frantically, must be thrown to the winds. Defiantly she shot Blake a glare from under her lashes, as if to remind him of common decency. His expression of intense fury left her breathless, every scrap of air rushing from her lungs.

'Let's get this straight. You call yourself Vaseux but you are a Bellamie?' he ground out, utterly disregarding her need for some peace and privacy.

'Yes!' she yelled over Luc's piercing cries with a defiant toss of her head. 'And proud of it!'

That told him, she thought grimly. And, not caring if Blake saw her breast or not, she undid her buttons and let Luc's rosebud lips brush her engorged nipple. After a moment or two of fussing around Luc latched on to her and his whimpers died away. There came the familiar tugging which normally relaxed her into a state of blissful pleasure. But not this time.

Not with the tall and menacing Blake looming over her,

his very stance a calculated threat as if he might be an avenging angel, determined to make her suffer because she bore her father's name.

Papa, you must have known this would happen! she mourned silently to herself. Why put me through this when you loved me?

Unhappily she cradled her child. Even the sight of Luc contentedly feeding, with all his red, screwed-up anger vanished and replaced by utter satisfaction, did nothing to ease her agitation. Something terrible was about to happen. Feeling nausea rise to her throat she choked it back. Bent her head and found refuge in kissing the pale silk of her son's white-blond hair.

But a relentless force dragged her gaze back, up to the scowling Blake. No, she thought, taken aback. Not scowling—riven with horror. Her tongue slipped nervously over her dry lips. If her hands had been free she would have put them over her ears to shut out anything he might say.

It was the sheer contrast of Blake's former pleasantness and this dreadful loathing that shocked her so much. Blake wasn't the vindictive sort. She'd instantly felt a bond with him. The kind that could, in other circumstances, have developed into a wonderful relationship.

And yet—

'I need to establish one or two facts,' he said, all ice and steel.

Unable to speak for the massive lump which sat resolutely in her throat, she clutched Luc more tightly as if he were her lifeline. What had her father done to deserve this? Why had the mention of his surname produced such a reaction?

'Like what?' she asked in a strangled kind of croak.

'Your father's full name.'

She trembled. 'Giles. Giles Bellamie.'

He inhaled sharply and she knew he recognised the

name because his face became drawn and his eyes darker than ever.

'And he is dead,' he stated bluntly, as if needing confirmation.

She winced. 'You know he is! I've scattered his ashes, haven't I?' she replied, feeling hysterical.

Why did he want to rub it in when he'd been so thoughtful before? She made an effort to even out her breathing. It was all over the place. She must stay calm for Luc's sake.

'Do you often interrogate women when they're breast-feeding?' she flung and had some satisfaction in seeing the colour flare across his high cheekbones.

'These are unusual circumstances.'

'Are they?' Her caustic glance swept across his uncompromising face.

'You want to trace your family?'

She narrowed her eyes. He sounded more under control now. But cold. So horribly cold in his manner.

'Depends,' she fended warily.

It seemed that he was considering various options. She watched him as he turned away and stared in the direction of the beautiful parkland beyond the drystone walls of the churchyard. The expansion of his back and the high carriage of his broad shoulders suggested that a conflict raged within him. Knots of sick anxiety twisted in her stomach. This was unbearable. Better to know everything than to carry this terrible suspicion about her father within her.

'Tell me what's wrong!' she demanded, her low voice vibrating with urgency. 'You know my father—'

He turned then, his expression haunted. '*Of* him.'

'And?' She could hardly breathe.

Slowly his glacial gaze devoured her, from the top of her shining blonde head to the tip of her chartreuse green pumps peeping from the gentle folds of her skirt. His mouth thinned in what she thought must be disapproval.

'You're very young,' he mused, his manner tight and shuttered as if he was repressing strong emotions. She thought he'd muttered, 'Too young,' under his breath but she wasn't sure.

'Twenty-five!' she supplied, a little indignant. 'Are you so old?'

'Twenty-eight,' he said in a clipped voice. 'And Luc is your own son, your own blood?'

Her mouth gaped. What was this? 'Of course! Do you think I carry another woman's baby around and feed him?' she flared, stung into fury by his inexplicable behaviour.

'I have to know!' he rasped.

The frostiness of Blake's expression—this man she'd instantly liked, whose son she'd thought so adorable— made her blurt out in self-pitying misery, 'Luc is all I have in the whole world, now!'

Immediately she wished she hadn't said that. It had sounded pathetic, as if she wanted to soften Blake up by appealing to him by means of her child.

True, there had been a tremor in his mouth as he'd briefly surveyed the swell of her breast and the blissful infant suckling there. But then his jaw had turned to concrete again and now his eyes were brooding on her— hooded, secretive, wary.

As if, she thought wildly, she might leap up and bite him and turn him into a vampire or worse.

'Your mother's dead?' he shot.

'Remarried, living in America and too busy living the high life to be bothered...' Irritably she checked her explanation and pruned in her mouth. 'What the hell has it got to do with you?'

'Everything.' He surveyed her for a moment then his head angled to one side speculatively. 'The name you used. Vaseux. Was that something your father adopted as a false identity?'

She shrank with horror, her eyes huge as her mind ticked off the reasons he'd think that. Crime. Fraud. Bigamy… Oh, this was ridiculous! There'd be a simple explanation. A misunderstanding.

'He was always Bellamie. It was my name too,' she muttered, still too shell-shocked to say any more.

'But…' He frowned. 'You said you weren't married,' he growled.

'No, I didn't. I said I didn't have a husband and I haven't,' she replied flatly. 'Not any more. I'm divorced.'

His head fell back in a gesture of despair. When he looked at her again she saw his teeth were clenched tightly together in an angry grimace.

'Does that mean that your husband was Luc's father?' he asked tightly.

Rage made her eyes glint with steely lights. What kind of person did he think she was? Maybe her life had been freer than that of most people she knew but she'd never been promiscuous or sexually irresponsible as Blake was suggesting.

The fury rose up in a huge, unstoppable surge. She was renowned for being amazingly easy-going and laid back in temperament until driven too far. And then sparks flew. They were about to ignite the touchpaper, big time, she thought grimly, heading straight for it.

'Are you trying to insult me or is it purely accidental?' she snapped.

The barb went home. He actually flinched. Or, rather, his mouth crimped in briefly before his very English self-control asserted itself again.

'I need to know if Luc is illegitimate,' he bit.

'Why?' she blazed. 'Don't you talk to the mothers of bastards?'

He flinched and went pale beneath his tan. 'It's not that!'

'Then what? Are you collecting gossip for the village magazine? Looking for fallen women to save?' she flung, getting well into her stride. 'Or doesn't the lord of the manor allow bastards in this village—?'

'That's enough!' Blake hissed, his entire body quivering with suppressed fury. 'Answer the question. Is he your legitimate son?'

'Yes!' she hurled back. 'Why is that so important to you? Tell me—or get the hell out!'

His hand shook slightly as it swept over his gypsy hair. He looked shell-shocked, his confident manner gone, his mouth compressed in a thin, hard line. And he seemed almost to shrink away from her as if she might be carrying the plague.

She gulped, even more apprehensive than before.

'I told you,' he grated harshly. 'I'm establishing facts.'

'Maybe. But for what purpose? You must tell me what's going on!' she cried in exasperation, so vehement in her movements that she dislodged Luc.

He protested long and loud. With her nerves skittering all over the place she quietened him and soon he was nursing again. That was when she looked up once more, her mouth set in a firm line of anger.

Again Blake appeared to be in the throes of a struggle with a powerful emotion. Twice he made to speak and stopped himself. Her fears increased. It was something to do with her father. And yet her Papa had been kind and generous, loving and loved!

Oh, Papa! she thought, dreading what was to come. A terrible revelation. Perhaps a criminal record, an injustice or maybe some misdemeanour in his youth with a village girl...

She closed her eyes in misery. Discovering a dark secret would destroy all her lovely memories of him and she wanted to hold on to them with a desperation that shook her to the core.

Blake had never known such indecision. There she was, the picture of aggrieved innocence, engrossed in the tender act of feeding her baby. Mother and child. A tiny defenceless baby, the rightful heir to Cranford.

He winced. Dear God! The shock had been more than he could bear for a moment. He'd seen his life—the life he loved—being brutally taken from him. The house, the land, his projects that he'd begun and those he'd successfully completed—all these would be no longer his to worry about, or his responsibility to guide to fruition.

He pictured Josef's face when he told him they were moving and his son's bewilderment as he struggled to understand what Granny had done and why they were leaving their beloved home, their friends, the life they had fondly imagined to be theirs by rights.

He felt the most terrible anguish tearing at his guts. It was a living nightmare. His whole life. All for nothing.

Fighting the knifing pains in his heart, he turned his back again on the touching scene as she gently rocked to and fro, an expression of deep anxiety creasing her clear forehead and drawing down those sensual lips into an expression of misery.

His brain seemed overloaded, every thought hurtling around and getting nowhere. First there had been the shock of meeting Giles's daughter, such a short time after his mother's revelation. Then the tender mother and child scenes. His sympathy for her. The terrible battle with his conscience. And, even more disturbing, the stirring—no, who was he kidding? The firing, the exploding, of his loins.

Incredible. She exuded sex from every pore, despite her motherly role. The sheer intensity of her sensuality had hit him like a physical blow, penetrating his cold indifference to women and setting him alight with almost unstoppable lust.

Every movement she made with that incomparable body, each wide-eyed glance and flicker of those impossibly long lashes, had attacked his celibate state and flung it so far into history that it was in danger of colliding with the ancient Romans.

His feelings alarmed him. By rights he should run a mile from someone who could affect him so strongly. He had wanted to take her in his arms. Kiss that soft, pliable mouth till they were both breathless. Crazy, unbelievable. Unwise even to dwell on such urges.

And yet, unable to stop himself from doing so, he glanced over his shoulder, hungry, aching for the very sight of her. His pulses leapt. The blood throbbed in his veins.

Her bent head shone like yellow glass in the sunshine. He took in the perfection of her skin, the small straight nose, those softly parted lips and desire rose within him as he'd never known it before. Hot, hard, urgent. Forget the Romans. He'd reverted to caveman levels. What the devil was happening to him?

Although he'd been determined not to let his gaze wander any further he found himself ignoring that decision. Hating himself, disgusted and torn with battles between his better nature and the coarser urges of his body, he let his tormented eyes linger on the flawless hill of her half-exposed breast.

And then, appalled and stunned by the sexual power she unknowingly wielded over him, he clenched his jaw and resolutely—with unbelievable difficulty—turned away again.

Struggled with his desire for a total stranger. His second cousin. Giles's daughter. A woman brought up by a man without morals. So what did that make her? It was inconceivable she could have remained totally untouched by her father's habits.

His entire system seemed to be in turmoil. But he knew one thing. This was when he should say to her, Your son owns this land and everything you can see. He owns a Tudor mansion, its mullioned windows and hammerbeam hall, the tapestries and treasures. He also owns stables, outbuildings, estate cottages and acres of land. Every month he will receive the rents that will assure his future and yours, as his legal guardian. You both have come into a fortune. And an ancient and historic dynasty.

The worst scenario of the evil Giles inheriting had been avoided by the man's death. Blake's duties were clear-cut. To announce Nicole's good fortune and bow out. Yet he couldn't bring himself to say the words.

Being a woman she couldn't inherit herself, but with eighteen years till Luc gained his majority she would be the one who ran the estate. And spent its money. But he knew next to nothing about her.

Except that she was beautiful and sexy. Earthy, even. Blake clenched his teeth, mentally killing his too-responsive leap of desire. This gut feeling for her was something raw and primal and utterly terrifying in its sweeping obliteration of his rigid self-control. It seemed that his safe, known world had been destroyed and with it his painfully acquired discipline over his wayward passions. His heart thundered. Had his mother's revelation released him from the strait-jacket of his emotions?

Was he the result of a union between two highly passionate people ruled by base needs? Fire was certainly coursing through his veins at this minute—and had been ever since he'd set eyes on Nicole.

He didn't like that loosening of control. Didn't know who he was any more. And that was terrifying, like being thrown into a deep hole and finding yourself forever falling.

Being freed from constraint was disturbing. Perhaps, he thought sourly, suppressing one's feelings had its compensations and could be a virtue after all.

He scowled at the ground. As for Nicole... What of her? She'd lived with her father. Couldn't have been ignorant of his ways—and yet she'd idolised him. Was that because she had similar tastes, or had she loved him *despite* his outlandish behaviour?

So many questions and no answers—though he needed them fast. Her character was the key to his next move.

Blake scowled, thinking of the way she'd responded to *him*, a total stranger, when his guard had slipped and he'd accidentally let his raw attraction surface. Her mouth had curved in a wanton smile, her eyes had issued an almost irresistible invitation. Which he'd almost grabbed with both hands.

It might be a mutual attraction. It might be her response to men. How would he know? He couldn't take risks with Cranford's future. If the land was mismanaged and drained of investment then the whole village would suffer. He had to know more about her before he took the irrevocable step of telling Nicole that her son was the heir.

Behind him he heard the sounds of her fingers fumbling with material. Buttons being done up. Life flared in his loins and he concentrated on timing some long controlling breaths even while his senses remained on high alert.

There came the zip of the baby bag. Her husky, deep-throated voice in that spine-tingling accent, speaking in French to the baby.

Here we are, my sweet. Let's get that bottom of yours sorted and then...

Her voice broke. He waited, the hairs rising on the back of his neck, tension in every sinew of his body as he strained to hear her low, secretive whisper in the language he knew as well as his own.

Then we'll get the truth from that man, even if I have to use all my wiles to do it!

Blake's eyes glittered. Fortunate that he had such good hearing. And that the Bellamie family—descended from a French ambassador who had 'gone native' in the reign of Elizabeth I and had been rewarded with Cranford for his loyalty—had not only adopted French names for the male heirs, but by tradition had sent them to France until they were fluent in the language.

So she wanted the truth. He'd tell her what he knew about her father, then, and see her reaction. Beneath those tears and the charm lay a strong will. He'd realised that when she'd defied him.

Unless he knew that she was of unimpeachable character he couldn't possibly hand over the house, or put the lives of people he cared about in her hands.

He thought of his mother, so close to death. His heart lurched with pity and he knew he couldn't tell her that the real heir had turned up. She would die a destroyed woman. It was his loving duty to protect her from harm at all costs. She had sacrificed everything for him. He could at least allow her to die content.

Filial love played tug-of-war with honour. And he found a way to satisfy both. He would deal with this later, he decided, putting off the evil hour. If he thought Nicole was worthy she would know the truth when she was ready to be told—and that would definitely be after his mother had died.

CHAPTER FOUR

WITH unusually clumsy hands Nicole finished changing Luc's nappy, her eyes warily flicking in Blake's direction. He'd keep. She had other priorities.

Tucking the now sleeping child into the sling, she fixed it in place and levered herself up from the bench, swaying a little as she did so. Her head felt full of cotton wool. Her stomach was running on empty.

Food, rest, and an explanation. In that order. Without the first two she'd never cope with the third.

'I'm going to the pub,' she announced to his uncompromising back. Her statement came out rather belligerently because she was trying to sound tough. No point in letting him think he could walk all over her. 'I'll ask them what *they* know about anyone called Bellamie.' He spun around with an intake of breath. She saw his eyes flicker in alarm and knew he hadn't liked that. Pleased with her tactic, she added, 'After that, I would like to meet up with you again. I have a right to know why you bear such hostility towards my father. And me.'

'You must come to my home, not the pub,' he grated.

'I'd rather eat worms,' she said tartly.

There was a flicker of something akin to alarm in his eyes. 'They're not on the menu. Nicole, you have to understand that this must be kept between ourselves,' he said ominously, striking fear into her again. His mouth twisted. 'No dirty washing in public. You know the expression?'

Mystified, she nodded. 'But what do you mean by it?'

There was a long tense pause. She could see that he was

steeling himself to say something he'd clearly prefer to keep to himself.

Eventually he said flatly, 'You are family.'

Her eyes widened in amazement. '*What* did you say?'

He stared then said with obvious reluctance, 'My name is Blake Bellamie. I am your second cousin.'

'*Cousin?*' she croaked.

There was no welcome. None of the easy charm she'd witnessed earlier. Just a coldly stated fact. She blinked, trying to gather her wits. He'd known they were cousins all the time he was interrogating her. And hadn't chosen to reveal their relationship.

'And when were you going to tell me this? Over coffee?'

He thought for a moment. 'Probably not.'

She gasped. That was unbelievable! 'How dare you? That's outrageous!' she stormed. It hurt even more because he'd been so kind before and they'd shared personal confidences. His change of attitude seemed almost like a betrayal. 'You knew I was upset,' she accused. 'You knew I wanted to find my family—' She paused. Drew breath. And hazarded, 'You only told me because I said I'd make enquiries in the pub, didn't you?'

'Yes. And you'll understand why in a moment. Where is your car?' he rapped out, grim-faced.

'By—by the post office—'

He nodded. Curtly. Strode off to the church without a backward glance and disappeared inside. Nicole wasn't sure what to do. Her legs wouldn't stop shaking. She could get in her car and vanish, keeping her father's memory safe. But, even as the idea came into her head, she knew with a heavy heart that for the rest of her life the mystery would fester in her mind.

She would wonder why a perfectly decent man—her kinsman, she thought in wonder—who loved his son and had shown consideration to a total stranger, should have reacted so adversely when he'd realised she was Giles Bellamie's daughter.

A cross-sounding child's voice penetrated her seething brain. 'But why, Daddy, why?'

Looking towards the church, she saw Blake pull a hand-kerchief from his pocket. He efficiently wiped Josef's cho-colatey face and hands. All the while he spoke quietly to his son. He seemed appeased because he grabbed his fa-ther's hand and trotted along beside him, seemingly un-aware of Blake's hard-jawed expression as he strode to-wards her.

'Hello,' chirruped Josef blithely. 'Hello, baby.' He pat-ted the sling with small, dimpled hands, his beaming smile a contrast to his father's cold reserve. 'Daddy says I can have ice cream for pudding when we get home—'

'Only if you eat your lunch in the kitchen with Cook,' Blake warned.

'Sometimes,' Josef said with a hugely artificial sigh, 'I wish we didn't have cream sofas.'

Despite her worries, Nicole couldn't help but smile. 'It'll be cosy in the kitchen,' she observed.

'Shall we go?' Blake suggested coolly. 'I'll direct you. It's not far. Josef and I will walk.'

'But—!' Josef began. And was silenced by his father's glare.

Dear heaven! she thought. Blake can't even bear to be in the same vehicle as me!

With Josef chattering with surprising knowledge about the plants and flowers beside the churchyard path, and with his occasional diversion to admire a gaudy beetle and a bustling colony of ants, she and Blake proceeded in stony silence to her car.

Remote and disapproving, he gave directions then col-lected Josef, who had been dangling perilously over a drystone wall above a sparkling stream, and headed off up the road.

It took her a while to unfasten Luc and secure him in the car. It took even longer for her to force herself to switch on the ignition. She felt weak as if all the stuffing had been ripped from her. It was obvious that she was heading for something unpleasant. She wished she'd never set eyes on the man she'd imagined to be a helpful stranger.

By the time she caught up with Blake and Josef they were walking through a large and imposing pair of wrought iron gates. Nicole slowed the car to a crawl, her eyes wide with astonishment as she scanned the beautiful parkland beyond.

Everything pleased her artist's eye. Post and rail fences edged the wide drive and sheep grazed on emerald-green fields studded with specimen trees. Hills clothed with woods rose in the distance and the scent of wild honeysuckle permeated the air, pouring through the car's open windows and filling it with fragrance.

Josef broke away from his father and clambered over the fence, waving frantically at a figure on horseback who was cantering in front of a stand of ancient oaks. As the rider came closer she saw that it was a woman—young and shapely.

Blake's wife? she wondered nervously. Someone else to slice her with a contemptuous glance. Her mouth set in a grim line. Well, she wouldn't put up with it! She'd done nothing wrong. There was no reason why Blake should be so unfriendly.

She revved up the car and shot forward to where Blake and Josef were talking to the slim, fair-haired woman. When Nicole killed the engine and jumped out she noticed the flash of annoyance in Blake's eyes. But she wasn't to be browbeaten.

'Hello,' she said to the woman, holding out her hand in greeting. 'I'm Nicole Vaseux. Blake and I are c—'

'This is Susie,' he broke in icily. 'She's just off.'

Susie looked faintly bewildered but hastily took Nicole's hand and shook it. 'How do you do?' She raised a questioning eyebrow at Blake.

'I know you're busy. See you later,' he said with a perfunctory smile.

'Daddy's in a funny mood. He's been walking all stiff and cross,' Josef confided to Susie. She did her best to hide a grin. 'Must go. 'Bye. Be good, Joe.'

'Goodbye, Mrs Bellamie,' Nicole said, taking a crafty shot in the dark.

'Susie,' Blake said in tones cold enough to freeze lava in its tracks, 'is a groom.'

It wasn't a word she'd come across before. Josef saw that and came to her rescue. 'She looks after the horses,' the little boy supplied, as Susie hurriedly left. 'Rides them. Keeps the tack clean. Shovels out the—'

'Thank you, Josef,' Blake said drily before his son became too explicit.

Nicole went pink. 'I thought she was your wife.'

'I don't have a Mummy,' Josef said amiably. 'She went off with the shuvver when I was little—'

'Chauffeur,' rasped Blake, scowling. 'Who told you that?'

'Oh, people,' Josef said vaguely. 'Can't remember, I talk to so many. I always wondered what a shuvver was. It's all right,' he added, seeing Nicole's look of alarm. 'I don't remember her. And Daddy makes a good Mummy. Then there's Cook and Maisie who cleans and—'

'Josef—' Blake said drily '—see how long it takes you to reach the front door from here. Take the short cut. I'll time you.'

'I expec' he doesn't like to remember,' Josef explained to Nicole.

But, as Blake opened his mouth with none-too-pleased an expression on his face, the little boy scampered away, apparently knowing when his father had reached the end of his tether.

Nicole said nothing. Although her gaze was directed towards Josef, who was disappearing into a vibrant stand of rhododendrons ahead, she was too busy digesting two new facts. Blake's wife had left him. And he seemed to have a battery of staff. What was his house like? It wasn't even in sight!

'You...'

'Yes?' he murmured.

She licked her lips, flushing at the sweep of his glance, which took her in from head to toe. There was something sexual about the curl of his mouth and it threw her off-balance for a moment. He was the most disturbing male she'd ever met in her life. Especially on an empty stomach. She must eat. Not indulge in idle chit-chat. But her curiosity won out.

'You *own* this incredible place?'

The curving line of his lips thinned. 'This is Cranford Hall. The Bellamies have lived here for centuries.'

'Oh! What about my father? Where did he fit in?' she began croakily, wondering about his part in this wealthy family of landed gentry. She couldn't imagine him here. Her father had never liked routine or convention. Was this why he had left such luxury? Before his work became widely known, he'd struggled to make a living. Her fingers fiddled nervously with her bracelets. Her throat had dried and the questions remained unasked.

Blake's brooding gaze slid over her once more and she fancied it lingered on the narrowness of her waist and the gentle swell of her hips. Again she felt that dangerous

lurch in her chest, a tightness that signalled her suscepti-
bility to his intense masculinity.

'You'll learn soon enough. You'll need to be sitting
down when you do,' he muttered alarmingly. 'Let's get
this over with as quickly as possible.' His voice gave no
clue to his feelings. 'Park by the main steps and go into
the hall. I'll join you there.'

'I must eat first,' she reminded him faintly.

He took one look at her white face and trembling lips
and frowned. 'Get in the passenger seat. You look terrible.
I'll drive. I don't want you lurching over the verge and
ruining it.'

Charming! she thought crossly. But did as he said. She
knew her limbs were turning to wobbly lumps of jelly and
she didn't want to risk an accident.

The car started up as soon as she had slammed the door.
With annoying ease, he persuaded her ancient and tricky
gears to obey the confident, sensitive flicks of his large
hands and they shot off up the drive.

They passed between avenues of rhododendrons and
azaleas then breath-stopping arches of cherry blossom.
Meadows sprawled beyond them, thick with bluebells,
wood anemones and snake's head fritillaries.

Her heart missed a beat. Like their meadow at home.

Without knowing she did so, she looked for acer trees
and found them. Pears, too, laden with blossom. There
were drooping, strap leaves where daffodils had once flow-
ered, seemingly acres of them. It must have looked spec-
tacular a month ago, she thought. A sea of nodding yellow
trumpets.

A sadness fell on her. All these were plants that her
father had insisted should be planted around the cottage in
France. He had loved it here, she thought with sudden
insight. And must have longed to return.

But he didn't. She shivered involuntarily.

'All right?' muttered Blake.

'No.' She wasn't going to pretend. 'Awful.'

'Nearly there.'

The house came into view. Tudor. She recognised the style from her Fine Arts course. Imposing golden stone, heavy chimney stacks and mullioned windows. It basked in the warm April light, masses of wisteria vying with a huge magnolia to hide the walls.

Below, in the borders against the house, she could see scarlet tulips amongst the shrubs and perennials, all of which she recognised. Her heart ached because her father had obviously lived here and had missed this house desperately. And she, too, felt her emotions stirred deeply, falling irrevocably in love with Cranford Hall.

'It's the most beautiful house I've ever seen,' she said, her voice soft with awe.

Blake glowered and swerved to one side, driving through a stone arch and into a paved yard surrounded by outbuildings. Without a word to her, he leapt out of the car and began unfastening Luc's baby seat.

Slowly, daunted by the size of the house and the revelations to come, she slid from her seat and meekly followed him as he manoeuvred the seat through a narrow plank door.

Her footsteps sounded deafening on the stone flag floor of the corridor but she controlled the urge to tiptoe. Blake paused and put his head around a door. From his softer body language—the lowering of his tense shoulders and the relaxing of his muscles—she realised that his son must be in the room. Perhaps it was the kitchen, she guessed, where Josef had been banished.

'Well done, Joe, you sped along like a bullet from a gun!' Blake declared, a smile in his voice. 'Special treat for pudding, I think, Mrs Carter. And could you rustle a lunch snack for me and my guest in the morning room?'

'Pleasure, Mr Blake,' came jolly, rosy tones of affection. 'Just be a jiffy.'

Mr Blake? Why use his first name like that? She frowned.

Following Blake blindly as he disappeared into a room with Luc, Nicole then remembered how her father had suggested that their once-a-week gardener in the Dordogne, who did all the heavy digging, should call him *Monsieur* Giles. A very English compromise with long-standing staff, she mused, thinking of the novels she'd read about the aristocracy in the UK.

Her father had never abandoned his past life, she realised, hunger and apprehension making merry with her stomach. All the signs had been there if only she'd known. Only a traumatic event must have kept him away.

An unbearable misery came over her and, closing her eyes for a moment, she stumbled. There was the sound of hurrying feet and she felt two strong arms come around her. Heat flowed from his hands. His breath mingled with hers.

She flung up her lolling head and met his dark commanding eyes. The room seemed to swirl about her and she was swept off her feet and found herself hovering in mid-air. Then she was being pressed against the living warmth of his chest where she could feel the thunderous beat of his heart. Before she had time to wonder why she felt the urge to put her arms around his neck, she had been deposited, none too gently, on a comfortable sofa.

'It's irresponsible of you to miss meals. You have a child to think of,' he snarled as if she'd done something to anger her.

Her head cleared. 'Luc!' she croaked, looking around wildly.

'Safe,' came the growled reply.

Following Blake's curtly angled head, she saw her son,

sleeping in blissful ignorance. The car seat had been placed in front of a table, evidently antique and of such highly polished oak that it must have had an army of servants working on it for a good few hundred years.

'I've never half-fainted before,' she mumbled crossly, struggling to sit up. 'But then I've never been bullied so unmercifully on an empty stomach.'

'I apologise if I have upset you,' he said stiffly.

'Upset?' She took a deep breath, her eyes like blue beacons of rage. 'I've recently lost my father. I have a small baby to bring up alone. I've travelled across France knowing that my father had kept his birthplace and nationality a secret from me. And then I come across you! Kind and sympathetic—till you knew who I was—and then you gave me the third degree and all but strip-searched me!'

She saw a flicker of acknowledgement set his stony face alive and knew that he would have gone that far if necessary. And her mouth tightened in contempt... Even as her body betrayed her by responding to the thought of Blake removing her clothes one by one. Dear heaven! she thought in horror. What had this man done to her sense of decency?

'I did apologise,' he said in a low hoarse tone. 'You'll understand my reaction when...' Pausing, he slid his tongue over his lips and inhaled deeply. 'Look, would you mind adjusting your skirt?'

Looking down, she blushed scarlet. It had rucked up to her thighs and had become caught beneath her body. With some difficulty she yanked it free, horribly conscious of Blake's hard-browed scowl.

Before she could retaliate by asking if he'd never seen legs before, there was a discreet tap on the door and a merry-looking lady, plump and dusted strategically with flour, came bustling in bearing a tray.

'I heard that you've come to scatter your father's ashes

here, and I'm ever so sorry.' The woman—whose voice she recognised as that of Mrs Carter, who'd spoken earlier—gave Nicole a genuinely sympathetic smile.

'Thank you.'

Shakily she smiled back, thinking that the bush telegraph worked fast here. But at least Mrs Carter wasn't looking at her as if she'd murdered half the inhabitants of Great Aston and pickled them in vinegar before feeding them to their dogs.

'I thought some home-made soup and hot rolls might be nice,' continued the comforting Mrs Carter. She flicked something beneath the laden tray and legs sprang out of it as if by magic. 'Then there's an assortment of cold meat and some hot chicken and mushroom pie with new potatoes. Home-made lemonade in the jug—and our own strawberries to follow.' She beamed at Nicole and then caught sight of Luc. 'Oh, what a poppet! Is that your baby?' she asked eagerly.

'Yes.' Nicole was grateful for a lull in the hostilities and her voice softened. 'He's called Luc.'

'Aaah!'

The woman's sentimental expression prompted Nicole to elaborate. 'He's seven weeks old.' And she glanced at Blake, wondering if she'd be going too far if she added, And he's legitimate. The warning look he gave her suggested that might be unwise so she turned her attention to Mrs Carter, who was cooing over little Luc.

'Pretty as a picture,' beamed the woman. 'And look, how extraordinary! His hair is as fair as the Bellamies!'

She felt Blake stiffen as she followed the cook's finger and saw that the woman was pointing to a series of oil paintings on the walls. Unaware of her surroundings up to now, Nicole realised that every painting depicted blond men, mostly from the nineteenth century. Presumably Bellamies. One even had eyes like her father's.

'But—' Nicole said, puzzled, and surveying Blake's Mediterranean colouring with curiosity '—not all of them are fair.'

'Always get throwbacks, dear,' Mrs Carter confided with a teasing wink at Blake.

He responded with a tight smile that didn't reach his eyes. 'Very true. Right, we'll make a start on this. Thank you, Mrs Carter. The lunch looks delicious,' he said in tones of polite dismissal.

Nicole realised that he had no intention of introducing her as a relative. She paled. A family secret. So she wasn't good enough? Or...her father wasn't. She bit her lip.

'Okeydokey.' The cook bustled to the door. 'I'll bring coffee when you ring. And some of your favourite chocolate thins.'

Blake muttered his thanks. 'Presumably Josef's been filling you in on the events of the morning, has he?' he asked lightly.

The cook gave a broad grin and nodded. 'While helping me finish making the cake for tea. As you can see.' Laughingly, she brushed at her hair with her sturdy fingers and a fine shower of flour formed a cloud around her face. 'Well, I must check if he's washed the pans properly—or maybe he's drowned himself and flooded the kitchen in the process!'

With another half-hearted smile Blake nodded and waited till she had rolled out of the room before ladling soup into a bowl and passing it to Nicole. The aroma was enticing and she dipped her spoon in it eagerly, giving herself up to the hedonistic pleasure of fresh, well-cooked food. It was rather, she thought ruefully, like a prisoner eating a last meal before being executed.

He ate little, she noticed—a few mouthfuls of the creamy watercress soup, a minute wedge of pie. Conscious of her need to fuel herself, she tucked in heartily.

It wasn't until she was well into her second bowl of strawberries that she realised he was watching her. Since her gaze was directed on her pudding at the time it rather shook her that it was a sudden pressure in her chest, not eye contact, which had alerted her to his attentions. Some power he had! she marvelled.

'You're ready to talk,' she said, her shaking fingers dabbing at her mouth with a linen napkin. 'I'm ready to listen.' Her eyes widened with apprehension as she met his gaze.

His chest rose and fell. There was an odd expression in his eyes. Sultry and intense. It made her head swim as if she'd drunk too much wine.

'Coffee,' he muttered and jerked to his feet, walking stiffly towards a tapestry bell pull. There was nothing sultry about him, after all, she realised. Just a brooding edginess, she decided, wondering how she could have misinterpreted his expression so badly.

A silence descended—hot, thick and suffocating. Nicole watched Blake striding up and down, her nerves in shreds. She could stand it no more. It would have looked silly if she'd paced up and down like him—however much she wanted to—so she went over to Luc and checked him then pretended to be sorting out the baby bag.

Surrounded by disposable nappies, wet wipes, little toys and changes of clothes, she heard Mrs Carter's knock with relief. Cups rattled on a tray accompanied by heavy footsteps and even heavier breathing.

'There we are! My, you've had a good meal. That's splendid! Never liked women who pick at their food. Shows a mean nature, I always—'

'Thank you,' Blake interrupted meaningfully.

Nicole had turned and was smiling at the cook, disarmed by the woman's jolly manner and total lack of ceremony. She guessed that Mrs Carter had been with the family a long time and felt able to state her opinions every now and then.

'It was a lovely meal. Thank you very much. I was starving.'

The cook beamed. 'No trouble at all. Don't tell Mr Blake—' she said, in a pretend whisper that he could hear perfectly well '—but I'd do anything for him, and that goes for his friends too.' Deftly, the trays were being swapped over with Blake's help. 'Oh,' sighed Mrs Carter, 'isn't it good to see a baby in the house? Those dear little hands...the dinky little nose...and the pretty toys... Does your heart good, doesn't it, Mr Blake?'

'Children are a source of great delight,' he agreed.

His tone had been soft as he eyed the sleeping Luc. Then a shadow fell over his face and he averted his gaze as if irritated by his thoughts. Nicole felt her stomach somersault. Perhaps he knew that her father had carried a rare disease that she and Luc could have inherited, she thought wildly, panic making her leap to all kinds of irrational explanations.

'Oh, well. Must get on and make some bread,' the cook said briskly. 'Ted's taken Josef off to sow lettuce, if you're wondering where he is.'

Nicole watched Blake open the door for his cook. Saw the true warmth of his eyes when he smiled his thanks. And then the shutters that closed his lively, expressive face the moment the door was shut.

Her huge eyes followed his every movement. That feral stride, so grim and determined, towards the sofa opposite her. The way he avoided meeting her gaze. The folding of his long, lean body when he sat down and the frown that brought thunder to his face.

When his chiselled lips parted to begin she gripped the arm of the chair in nervous anticipation and tried to calm the tumult in her mind. This was it. The explanation.

CHAPTER FIVE

I COULD get used to this, Nicole thought, luxuriating in perfumed suds. She closed her eyes, quite exhausted, and let her mind drift.

There had been a mistake about her father, of that she was sure. The stories Blake had told her an hour earlier bore no relation to the man she knew at all. And she'd let him know that, in no uncertain terms. Well, she'd shouted at him, if she was honest. But how dared he make such ridiculous and disgusting accusations? Still, they were so silly that she could rest in peace.

Under the circumstances, it had surprised her when he'd offered hospitality. Perhaps he was worried she'd contaminate the villagers, she'd thought tartly.

However, since she hadn't booked accommodation for that night, she'd agreed to stay in the manor house. Providing Blake talked about non-controversial topics like religion, politics, capital punishment and the state of the economy rather than the vile things he'd accused her father of doing.

'You don't believe me,' he said flatly after relating his improbable stories about her father's sexual rampages as a teenager.

Her eyes flashed a warning. 'If I weren't so angry I'd be laughing. My father was amiable and easy-going. He lived for his work, his painting.'

'And sex.'

'Hardly. He had a couple of female friends after my mother left, yes. Nothing wrong in that. Consenting adults—'

63

'Why did your mother leave?'

Nicole made a face. 'She met someone richer and more famous! My father was still struggling to make his name and she was fed up with poverty. Some women can't handle being poor,' she said defiantly when he frowned.

'I know,' he said tightly and she wondered about that. He would have been wealthy all his life, surely? 'Why did she marry him if he was so poor?'

'A misunderstanding,' she replied sadly. 'When they first met, he had a Bentley and some valuable personal jewellery. Mother told me she'd been misled by this until he started selling things to pay the rent.'

Blake pursed his lips. 'Money slipped through his fingers—'

'No, it didn't!' she cried indignantly. 'He saved hard. Went without so I was clothed and fed—'

'But he indulged himself too,' Blake growled. 'You can't tell me that your father was never drunk.'

'No, I can't,' she conceded. 'But—'

'I thought so!' Blake said in triumph.

'Once and once only!' she defended. 'And with good reason!'

She couldn't speak for a moment. It hurt to remember. The shock of hearing about her father's terminal illness had stunned her into silence and for a moment the world had stopped turning.

She pictured him—tragic, wracked with pain, his voice breaking as he'd gently given her the news. Anger surged. What did this cushioned, protected lord of the manor know about despair and tragedy?

'My father was drunk that one time because he had the hardest thing in the world to tell me,' she gritted, her eyes flashing with fury. 'He wasn't thinking of himself. Only me. He knew how I'd feel.' She flung back her head, misery and rage tightening the muscles of her small, defiant face. 'He told me that he only had a short time to live. I think anyone's entitled to get a little drunk under those circumstances, don't you?'

Blake didn't look convinced by her explanation. 'Alcoholics are skilled at keeping their weakness from members of their family—'

'He was not an alcoholic!' she cried hotly.

He shrugged as if her opinion couldn't be trusted. 'Or deviant? You don't recall any wild parties?'

She'd felt like hitting him. 'Never deviant! How *dare* you!'

'No parties?' he drawled.

'Are they illegal now?' she snapped.

His eyebrow hooked up cynically. 'Depends what went on.'

'You could have invited the vicar,' she snapped. 'Sure, we had parties. Noisy ones. If you call music and singing and laughter and excited chatter "wild" then yes, we had parties like that! Never anything bad. People brought their children. Do you think they'd subject them to anything indecent?' she cried indignantly. 'In all the years I knew him he never hurt anyone or anything—'

'Your mother wasn't so thrilled with him,' Blake pointed out, his expression scathing.

'If I were mean-minded,' she answered sharply, 'I could say the same thing about your ex-wife. And my ex-husband. But does that make us monsters?'

He gave a little smile of grudging admiration, his glittering eyes boring deeply into her as if they intended to penetrate the whole of her brain and lay it out for analysis. 'If you're so feisty after harrowing experiences and an exhausting journey,' he mused surprisingly, 'I wonder what you're like when you're on top form?'

'Dynamite.' So beware, her silvered eyes told him.

'Yes... I can believe that.'

The low husk of his voice curled into her and the inky blackness of his eyes created havoc throughout her body. She could feel his sexual aura drawing her inexorably towards him. So she folded her arms as a barrier between them. Then realised that the action had pushed her breasts into greater prominence than was wise. And that was when she flailed around for some way to escape and asked if she might have a bath and a rest.

With a sigh, she slipped deeper into the foam, letting her body float in the enormous Victorian tub. The bathroom was the most opulent she'd ever seen, with rich and heavy gold curtains at the window, looped up with heavy tasselled ties.

When she'd walked in her bare feet had almost disappeared into the cream carpet and she was looking forward to snuggling into one of the giant bath towels, which were as soft as a baby blanket. Freed from her fears that her father had done something dreadful, she could now relax. Blissful music from a discreetly hidden stereo filtered into her semi-consciousness.

After this glorious soak she would draw the hangings of the four-poster bed and shut out the world till it was time to feed Luc, who was currently chortling away in one of Josef's old cribs. She glanced over at it with admiration. It was a family heirloom and sixteenth century, judging by the coat of arms on it.

She smiled. How the other half lived! But she had no reason to stay. She had what she'd come for. The link had been made with her father's family. The mystery was solved.

There had clearly been a falling out between her father and someone. Stories had been invented by Blake's family to explain why a Bellamie should want to leave the paradise that was Cranford Hall. Blake had even admitted that he'd never known her father, who'd apparently disappeared one night at the age of twenty or so. Though Blake wouldn't reveal who'd fed him those terrible stories.

Instead, he'd personally escorted her up to a suite of rooms in the west wing and had said that he'd come for her at seven to take her down to dinner.

'I can find my own way,' she'd said huffily.

'Please wait here,' he'd insisted. 'I would be failing in my duties as a host if I left you to wander the corridors and possibly get lost.'

Odd that, she mused, clambering out and cuddling into the towel. He'd been quite tense at that moment. It was almost as if he didn't trust her not to poke about in the other rooms and perhaps slip a few antiques into the baby bag!

'Well, Blake Bellamie—' she said cheerfully, vigorously rubbing herself dry '—by this time tomorrow I'll be on my way home. And you and your precious family can keep your prejudices and nasty minds because I want nothing to do with you. Despite the fact—' she added ruefully, slowly studying her ripe and totally wasted curves '—that you are the sexiest man I've ever seen.'

Her breasts swelled before her eyes. Hazily she watched her nipples harden and she groaned at the liquefying of her loins. She throbbed there. And wanted Blake at that moment more than she'd ever wanted a man before.

Stunned by the power he had over her, even when he wasn't anywhere near, she lifted her head and stared blindly at the full length window across the room. Then her eyes focused on something moving in the far distance.

Wrapping the towel securely around herself, she hurried over. Someone was riding like the wind across the park. A tall dark figure on a gleaming black horse. She quivered.

Blake.

The flames rose in her body, consuming her. And she berated herself for falling for such a hackneyed, romantic image. Man on horse. A symbol of power and mastery, physical energy and virility.

And Blake would be virile. All that unleashed vitality. The tightly controlled emotions. In bed, a man like that would be a tiger set free from a cage. Little shivers ran up and down her body, electrifying it. And she felt ashamed of her thoughts.

She'd been untouched for too long and was fantasising. Blake didn't even like her. Every time he'd come near he'd been tense with suppressed anger because she'd sullied his house by being the daughter of the family scapegoat.

Dinner would be a cold and icy affair. She sighed, turning from the window and determinedly banished the distant figure from her mind.

Beginning to prepare for Luc's needs, she told herself that she'd eat in silence, go to bed immediately after, and leave the next morning for the long journey back to France without saying goodbye. He didn't deserve courtesy. Besides, he'd be glad to see the back of her.

His entire body tingled from the elation of his ride. Unusually, it had taken a long time to rid himself of his pent-up feelings. Nicole had wormed her way into the very tissues of his body, it seemed, and all but pulped his brain. What a fool he was to lust after her when he'd remained indifferent to dozens of willing women far more suitable!

But she was a woman who knew all about pleasure. You could see that in the sway of her body, the knowing, flirty glances and the provocative pout of her lips. She'd be unbelievably abandoned, he'd thought.

And had been obliged to wipe her from his mind and straining manhood by galloping as far as the outskirts of Broadway.

Pleasantly exhausted, Blake spent an hour with his

mother telling her the events of the day—leaving out any mention of Nicole at all, of course.

Mrs Carter and the rest of the staff had been puzzled by his request that his mother should not know about their unexpected guests, but he knew they'd carry out his wishes.

It was a slight risk having Nicole around for the night but it was better than having her talking to the villagers. And despite her spirited defence of her father she'd looked tired and drawn. The main thing was that he should keep her from wandering about and stumbling on his mother's suite of rooms by accident.

He didn't have the heart to send Nicole on her journey without time to recover. It was the least he could do for a member of his family. A new mother with a baby to manage. A woman who aroused terrible longings in him...

Impatiently he blanked out his mind, scowling as he began to dress for dinner. She'd seemed to accept the situation. He'd shown her the family tree. For a moment he'd had to put a hand out to steady her because she'd gone white and had swayed at the sight of the neat square which had been cut in the parchment where her father's name should have been. He'd always been told the genealogist had made a mistake in drawing up the tree but now he knew that Giles had been deliberately removed.

His arm had slid around her shoulders and he'd almost given in to his compulsion by hugging her to him in sympathy. But she'd drawn in a massive breath and shrugged him off, noting coldly that they had great-grandparents in common.

'Yes. My grandfather and yours were brothers. Our fathers were first cousins,' he replied.

'Until my father was obliterated from your lives,' she muttered, her face set in mutiny. 'Someone in your family is lying, Blake! Someone who wanted him gone!'

That shook him for a moment. But he couldn't believe that of his mother, not when she knew she was dying.

'I can understand why you want to believe that. But it's not true. Accept it, Nicole.'

'I can't!' she cried, her eyes haunted.

It was hard, not touching her then. She needed comfort. Somehow he steeled himself to resist. 'Give me your address,' he suggested instead. 'We'll keep in touch.'

And she did. It was his intention that some time in the future he'd invite her over to see if she could be trusted with Cranford. But for now it was better for his mother's sake that she stayed away.

'Hello, Daddy!' A small whirlwind flew through the door and launched itself at his thoughtful figure. Deftly he caught Josef and flung him, laughing, on the bed where they wrestled for a bit.

'Don't you ever knock?' he grumbled amiably, escaping the giggling Josef. He sucked in his lean, muscled stomach and tucked in his shirt.

'Why? Nobody's in here, only you!'

It flashed into his mind that he could have been making love to Nicole. For a split second he saw her lush body writhing invitingly on his bed and then he fiercely rejected the idea. Though his arousal was less easy to dismiss.

'You're in your best suit,' mused his infuriatingly observant son. 'Does that mean Nicole's here for dinner? Can I stay up too?' he asked eagerly.

'You've eaten. I saw you demolish a huge plate of spaghetti bolognaise, two crusty rolls collapsing under mountainous lumps of butter and two portions of strawberries.'

'I am a bit full. I could watch you eat, though!' Josef attached himself like a leech to Blake's leg. 'Oh, please! Please, oh please!' he begged, for all the world like a silent movie heroine pleading with wicked Sir Jasper. 'I'll tidy my room. I'll even *wash* again—'

'Good grief! That's a bit drastic!'

Grinning, Blake hobbled over to the mirror, dragging Josef with him as he went. He tried to concentrate on getting his tie to sit right. His fingers seemed to be clumsier than usual. And why the heck *was* he making such an effort? He thought of being with Nicole. Candles on the dinner table. Intimacy...

'I'll ring ChildLine,' Josef threatened, still casting himself as the victim. 'Show them my wet pillow where I cried myself to sleep—'

'Idiot!' he said affectionately. Suddenly Josef's presence seemed a good idea. Blake yanked at the stubborn tie and started again as his son began to sob unconvincingly. 'Boo hoo isn't a very good impersonation of someone who's upset,' he drawled, fighting his laughter. And went in for some bargaining. 'Tidy your room and do your teeth for a week without complaining. Then you can come with me to collect Nicole for dinner—'

'I could practice making polite conversation for a bit,' Josef said craftily.

Blake nodded 'After that, you're going to bed without arguing and you'll tuck yourself in.'

Blake felt rather pleased with himself. Josef would remind him of his fatherly role and wipe out all thoughts of an evening's seduction by the earthy Nicole. He cleared his throat, which seemed to have become husky and finished dressing.

'You're making an awful fuss tonight. You've brushed your hair four times,' his son accused.

'It's a mess. That's why,' Blake growled, irritated to be found out. He flung the brush down, impatient with himself. 'Come on. Let's go.'

'Piggyback!' demanded Josef and, to his surprise, his father readily agreed.

Jogging along the corridor with his son's two bony

knees crushing his upper ribs, Blake reflected—not entirely with relief—that their arrival would kill even the lustiest woman's desire for casual sex.

Hopefully it would kill his, too. He'd never wanted a one-night stand before. Had never imagined that he could desire a woman so fiercely that he could contemplate satisfying his lust in a no-strings-attached, rollicking orgy of mind-blowing sex.

Hell. He was getting hot again. He had to get a grip.

'Come on, Daddy!'

To his surprise, he discovered he'd stopped. And his jockey was urging him on with impatient whipping movements. Blake felt the warmth of his son's body through his jacket, the sweet breath that fanned his face and the pressure of a soft cheek against his.

This was more precious, more lasting and more worthwhile than anything in the world. Overcome with love for Josef, he threw back his head in a magnificent whinny, pawed the ground and took off at top speed.

He and his jockey roared with laughter as they careered madly from side to side and occasionally jumped an imaginary fence. By the time he knocked on the guest room door they were both breathless and in hysterics. Josef was clinging to Blake's neck—nearly throttling him—and, like him, was quite helpless with laughter.

Nicole heard them coming long before she heard the rap on the door panel. It gave her time to compose herself. And to check her appearance in the mirror.

Alarmed, she saw that the flush on her face almost matched the scarlet of her dress. In panic, she wished she'd worn something more modest. It looked as if she was putting herself up for grabs. She hesitated, torn between answering the door and dashing back for a wrap to cover her almost bare shoulders. And the even more daring cleavage.

But Josef was shouting outside and so she grabbed Luc

and hurried to the door. Blake would be too taken up with managing his son to disapprove of the outfit she'd worn so many times without comment... Until that farewell dinner in France, she remembered in dismay, as she opened the door. And that was when she knew she'd made a mistake.

At first Blake's appearance made her go weak at the knees. Laughing at his son, his face wreathed in smiles and with that devastatingly infectious grin, his joy went straight to her heart and dug a little place for itself there.

Leaning over Blake's shoulder, Josef was a smaller version of his father—tumbled black curls rioting everywhere, black brows and eyes, mischief dancing in every line.

But Blake's countenance had become dark and scowling the moment he set eyes on her. Sliding his son to the ground, he even took a step backwards after flashing a cursory glance up and down her body. His mouth thinned. He narrowed his eyes. Clenched his fists.

Nicole's spirits fell. He thinks I'm parading myself. That I'm cheap, she thought in dismay. And cradled Luc protectively over her offending bosom.

'Are you ready?' he asked in a husky growl.

She gulped, her eyes huge. And opted for a cover-up. She couldn't nurse Luc like this all evening! She'd never be able to eat a thing!

'I—I have a wrap to collect.'

His head jerked in a nod of approval. 'We'll wait.'

Perhaps she ought to pull on a fleecy sweatshirt, she thought moodily. Or an anorak and a woolly scarf plus a duvet. Then he couldn't complain.

She groaned at her stupidity. Why had she worked through every item she'd brought and yet opted for this outfit, when she could have chosen something less in your face?

Vanity, she sighed, and carefully placed the wriggling

Luc on the clothes-strewn bed. She knew she looked good in the slim-fitting red dress. Aware that it would be a difficult evening, she'd wanted to feel her best. To impress the hell out of Blake and make him respect her. Instead, she'd ended up making herself look over-eager. Crossly she rummaged in her case for the silk wrap, conscious that Josef had bounced into the room.

'Wowee!' she heard the little boy's voice pipe up behind her bent back. 'You're as messy as me!'

'Joe!' barked Blake.

Flushing with embarrassment, she turned, wishing they hadn't seen the evidence of her dithering over what to wear.

'I've never eaten anywhere this posh,' she explained hurriedly, neatly dodging the truth.

'It's only Dad. Mind you, he *is* all done up like a dog's dinner tonight,' agreed Josef equably.

Her glance flew to Blake's. Inky-black met anxious blue. And she felt as if she'd been electrocuted. Delicious tingles were reaching hitherto unknown parts of her body. She could hardly breathe.

'He looks very nice,' she said in a garbled croak, making the understatement of the year.

Nice! Edible, more like it. Groomed, beautifully turned out in a soft charcoal suit that had been cut to flatter his broad shoulders, well-developed chest and slim waist and hips. A turquoise shirt and emerald tie deepened his tan. He was gorgeous and she felt heartily relieved that Josef would, it seemed, be dining with them.

'Shall we go?' Blake suggested loftily, scooping up Luc from the bed.

Her initial protest at the cavalier takeover of her child died on her lips. Luc had spent so much time with her— and her alone—that he didn't go to strangers readily. And yet her son was cooing merrily to Blake, another convert to the wretched man's charm!

Still, she thought, tossing the silk around her shoulders and drawing the wrap closely around her, Blake toting a baby was less of a sexual danger to her wayward hormones. Then, as she headed off down the corridor with Josef on one side and Blake on the other, she realised that she was wrong. Again. Blake's tenderness, his air of gentle protection and the sight of his huge hands carefully cradling her beloved son, combined to turn her heart over.

Help, she wailed silently. And help came.

'It's been nice weather today, hasn't it?' ventured Josef cheerily, hopping up and down beside her as they reached the landing.

She wondered if this was his version of polite conversation. 'Just lovely,' she agreed, glad of the child's presence. And, seeing his joyful face, she impulsively reached out and took his hand.

The little boy looked up at her with blinding delight. 'Have you come far?' he enquired as they began to descend the grand staircase.

Nicole hid a giggle. 'From France. A long way,' she replied.

Josef broke away from her, straddled the banister, slid down to the bottom and then raced up the stairs to them again.

'Much traffic?' he asked politely.

She met Blake's eye, caught its amused gleam, and they both convulsed with laughter. So much so that she had to sit on the stairs.

'What? What did I say?' demanded the perplexed Josef.

'Oh, sweetheart!' she said, hoping she hadn't hurt his feelings. He tucked himself next to her and she put her arm around him lovingly. 'It's... Well, you sounded so grown-up but not like *you* at all. Though it was a very good…er…'

'Impersonation of adults at a cocktail party,' Blake supplied.

'Yes, absolutely brilliant,' she agreed, seeing the little boy brighten. She got to her feet and took his hand again.

As they entered the sitting room, she thought contentedly that the evening was turning out better than expected. It was a long time since she'd felt so much at ease.

'Time for your story,' Blake said softly to his son. He brought Luc over and tucked him in a heap of cushions next to Nicole.

Josef looked appealingly into Blake's eyes, heaved a huge, wistful sigh and said hopefully, 'If you're ever thinking of getting a new Mummy for me—'

'I'm not. Did you know about the little boy who found a baby dragon in his pocket and it was crying because it was stuck to a half-sucked boiled sweet?' Blake said with a masterly diversion tactic.

The story unfolded with much drama and over-acting till she was consumed by giggles like Josef. The unlikely tale ended on a hilarious high note and gales of laughter. Then, unbidden, Josef ran over to kiss her goodnight, pecked Luc on the cheek and flung his arms around his father who hugged him hard.

'I love you, Daddy.'

'I love you too,' Blake said huskily.

The adoration in Blake's eyes as he followed his son's exuberant, cartwheeling departure made a lump come to her throat. This family evening had been a revelation. A startling insight into Blake's character.

She was overwhelmed by a need for him to like her. To accept the truth about her father, instead of believing those vicious rumours. Blake wasn't a hard and vindictive man. He'd just been misinformed. His family had made out that her father was some kind of monster and Blake had believed the stories unquestioningly. That was understandable. Why should he do otherwise?

But she couldn't leave it like that. There and then, she decided to stay in the area till she'd convinced Blake that her father should be reinstated on that wretched family tree. And, she vowed, she would insist that a memorial plaque be made to join the others in the church, which apparently recorded the existence of every Bellamie descendant since the fifteen-hundreds. She smiled, feeling a warm glow as she imagined herself unveiling that plaque...

'Shall we go in to dinner?' Blake murmured softly.

There was an unnerving glitter in his eyes. Just a reflection of the chandelier, she was sure, but for a moment the illusion of intense interest in them had unsettled her. She swallowed, telling herself to stop being so fanciful.

'Yes. Sure. Is...anyone else joining us?' she asked, her heart thumping madly at the thought of eating with him alone.

'Just us. Is that a problem?'

She looked at him but couldn't hide her doubts. 'N-no—'

His mouth curved in a heart-stopping smile. 'We could make polite conversation like Josef. The weather—'

'The traffic!'

She laughed in delight at his chuckle and blessed Josef for lifting the atmosphere between herself and Blake. At least, she thought, holding Luc closely as they headed for the door, she could always fuss over her baby if there were any sticky moments.

But she found herself reckoning without Mrs Carter, who surged in with starters of crab, leek and Gruyère tart and whisked the gurgling Luc off before Nicole could voice more than a token protest.

'He'll need a feed in an hour or so,' she reminded Blake.

'No problem. But for a while you can have a break from being a mother.' Blake's eyes kindled and she felt her heart bumping erratically. 'I want to thank you,' he went on. 'I'm grateful for your tact with Joe over his efforts at polite conversation.'

She beamed. That was a safe subject. 'I couldn't hurt his feelings.' Her voice softened. 'He's terrific, Blake. Very loveable. I only hope Luc grows up to have half his spirit and lust for life.'

He poured himself a glass of wine, nodded when she refused one and filled a tumbler of mineral water for her. 'He likes you a lot.'

Those dark, intensely brilliant eyes were fixed on her and destroying her brain cells again. She sighed. 'I feel enormously honoured. I don't imagine he suffers fools gladly.'

Like his father, she almost added, but restrained herself, not wanting to spoil the amicable atmosphere.

There was a long pause during which Blake studied her thoughtfully. 'No. He doesn't.'

It was a small victory, getting him to admit that, but it meant a great deal to her. She had won over Josef without any effort on her part. Now she needed to bridge the chasm between herself and Blake. That might take some doing— but she had to gain his trust if she was to convince him of her father's good character.

He bent his head and kept his attention on transferring a forkful of crab and pastry to his mouth. In the flickering candlelight, with the silk shawl draped over her smooth shoulders and her face alive with tenderness for his son, she looked too good to be true. Unbelievably beautiful. Huge intensely blue eyes, a sweet face and a mouth made for kissing. All that he could have handled—blocked out, with an effort of will. But she'd bonded immediately with

Josef, which made her special. And for a short time during the story-telling Blake had felt a pang of longing for a deep relationship with a woman who could instantly fit into his family set-up. That period before dinner had been how he'd always dreamed a family should be. A relaxed atmosphere in which laughter and warmth and love could flourish.

'Not too windy today, was it?' he heard her say.

He looked up and laughed. 'I'm sorry,' he said, his eyes twinkling. 'I was miles away.'

'Miles away... Hmm. Much traffic?' she teased.

He grinned and saluted her wit with his raised glass. 'Only in my head. You know the next stage of the conversation, don't you?' Pushing his empty plate away he leaned forward, trying not to notice the rise and fall of her breasts. 'Tell me about yourself.'

Her eyes glowed brightly as if he'd given her the opportunity she'd craved. OK, he thought, sell yourself.

And all through the main course he listened and prompted, encouraging her to reveal more of her true nature. Increasingly impassioned, she spoke of the small cottage, her father's modest fame, her own work in restoring antique ceramics.

He looked at her hands—slender, delicate, sensitive. He went to the sideboard and brought over a Lalique vase with a small chip in the base, which she handled with loving care, stroking it sensually.

In his fevered imagination he could feel those hands caressing him. And, as she described how she would repair the vase, he almost believed her words became slower and more slurred to match his own drugged senses.

'You inherited your love of beautiful things from your father,' he said throatily. And a sour voice reminded him that this had included beautiful women by the dozen. Giles had loved women but he had also abused them. The highest and lowest pleasures of the flesh.

'I hope I've inherited his nature, too. His kindness. Tolerance. Boundless hospitality.'

Her worship of her father shone through everything she said. But those traits she'd described could be taken too far.

'He was very much a party animal from what you've said,' he probed.

'I'll say!' Her eyes sparkled with enthusiasm. 'He loved people and they loved him,' she said, naively innocent of the slant he might put on that remark. 'There was a constant flow of friends visiting with their families. They were always welcome.'

'Tell me more about the parties. What they were like.'

Her voice became wistful. 'We'd sit late into the night beneath the stars, children lolling on parents' laps, vigorous discussions raging around the table, punctuated by laughter.' She smiled. 'I adored it.'

'You like dancing? Music?'

Her eyes glistened. 'Oh, yes! I'd dance till I dropped sometimes. Music sets me on fire. It has the power to make me cry or laugh. We would all abandon ourselves to it during those parties.'

'Oh?' His eyebrow lifted and in that 'oh' was a wealth of meaning.

'Not the way you're thinking!' she declared indignantly. 'We just let ourselves respond to the rhythm, whether it was fast and furious or slow and dreamy. Children, adults, grandparents...' Scathingly she accused, 'You wouldn't know about that. You've probably never done anything reckless or spontaneous in your life!'

'I have responsibilities,' he snapped, stung by the truth of her words.

'But you need to live, too!' she declared passionately, her face alive with vital energy.

Yes. He did. Increasingly so. All his life he'd been mindful of his position. Careful not to say or do the wrong thing. And now Nicole was taunting him with her freedom from restriction, unwittingly goading him to crush her in his arms and make frenzied love to her.

No wonder he desired her. She was everything he longed to be. She epitomised the kind of person he'd always been, deep down, beneath the self-control. At that moment he would have willingly exchanged life-styles.

There was a striking contrast between her description of carefree living and his own sober upbringing. So many times he'd balked at the straitjacket of being the 'son' of an English gentleman. And more than ever he envied her the freedom he'd been denied.

Growing in confidence, she became more expansive, less inhibited in her movements. A glow lit her eyes. And he was mesmerised by her, drawn to her because of everything she represented. And wanted.

'I beg you—' she said softly, perhaps sensing the softening of his brain '—ask people here about my father. Keep an open mind till you have evidence of his supposed wickedness.'

Her sweet, hopeful smile would melt the stoniest heart, he thought, sternly resisting such a fate. She drew in a deep breath and he felt first a kick of need and then pure anger. She must know how her body moved, he thought cynically, loathing women who used sex to get their own way.

And yet, despite knowing that she was deliberately enticing him, his anger turned to a hunger, a longing to possess part of this free-living woman who had lived the kind of life he had always yearned for.

She was offering. Why not take?

Blake sat back in his chair, his expression giving no hint of the passions that raced through his body. But she was destroying his control inch by inch, leaning forward in her eagerness to paint her father white, gesticulating in a typically Gallic way, graceful, fiery and intense.

All he could think of was touching that silken skin. Cradling her delicate face in his hands. Drawing her close and feeling the soft curves melt against him and her lips parted for his inevitable kiss... Surrendering at last to the need that raced excitedly through his body.

'Blake?'

He blinked. Felt close to exploding. Had to move. Abruptly he got up and removed their plates, carrying them to the sideboard.

It had been an error, going close to her for that brief moment to pick up her plate. She had looked up at him and murmured her thanks, her eyes two deep silver wells in the candlelight, and he'd almost jumped in head first to drown a happy man.

The memory of her perfume stayed with him as he briskly cleared the vegetable dishes. She didn't offer to help but remained in her seat looking rather forlorn. An act again? he wondered savagely. Grimly controlling his urge to haul her up and rain a torrent of kisses on that pouting, lush mouth, he cut them both a slice of raspberry pavlova. He slid hers in front of her then regained his seat, moving like a stiff automaton because if he allowed himself any fluidity at all he'd be surrendering to the little voice inside his head which kept saying, *Respond. She's interested. Go for it.*

Discipline prevailed. The meringue tasted like sandpaper to him but it was probably excellent as usual.

'You weren't listening. I've been boring you,' she said unhappily, her pudding untouched.

Boring him! If only. He registered the sexy pout of her

mouth and felt angry that she was able to affect him so deeply.

'I heard every word.'

Keeping his head down, he scooped up some raspberries and tried to look as if he was enjoying them.

'Then you'll understand—' she said, her voice unfairly throaty and low and making a mess of his intentions to stay detached '—why I can't allow you to think—let alone say—those awful things about my father.'

He had to get up again. Strode towards the window and flung the curtains back, then the French doors, to let in the starlit night. He breathed the air for a moment till his head cleared. She was using her femininity to persuade him, he thought angrily. Flirting with him. Lowering her voice and occasionally her eyes to weaken his resistance and get her own way. Meaningless tricks. And he was falling for them, big time.

'My source is unimpeachable. My source would not lie,' he said firmly.

He heard the scrape of her chair. The sound of her feet in the gloriously feminine high heels tapping towards him. And his loins melted.

'Well, something's wrong because I know I'm not lying!' she cried fervently, just inches behind him. 'I knew him and you didn't. I'm more likely to be right about him!'

Her breath teased the hairs on the back of his neck. If he turned around he knew he'd take her in his arms and make an utter fool of himself. He tried to make his addled brain focus more clearly. It was clear that she genuinely believed her father to be a good man. That left him with a dilemma. To accept her at face value and question his mother's version of events, or to keep silent as he'd intended until he knew more about her.

Her hand touched his arm and he stiffened automatically.

'Please, Blake,' she breathed jerkily. 'I know you don't like me, but you're a good man and I'm sure if you think about this dispassionately you'll realise I—I...'

He flung his resolutions to the wind and turned around in a violent movement. Nicole's upturned face swam before his eyes. Unable to stop himself, he took a step closer. Caught hold of her arms in a fierce grip.

And saw the drowsy flutter of her lashes, the sultry pout of her mouth as she signalled with every languid bone in her body that she, too, was aroused. He frowned, registering the shortness of his breath.

'Nicole,' he grated harshly. And he knew he'd reached the point of no return.

CHAPTER SIX

SHE couldn't move. Of course she'd heard of the *coup de foudre*—that bolt from the blue that could strike unexpectedly and fatally. But she'd never believed that instant attraction could possibly exist until now.

Not this deep, this obliteratingly single-minded, need to touch someone, be with them, follow their every move.

Alarmingly, her quest was being wiped from her mind by the urgency of her need. It was a wonderful feeling and her entire body was driving her to give in to the inevitable consequences, to strain forward and kiss Blake's stubborn, grim mouth until it softened. Until he flung away his rigid manner and let blood flow into his veins.

She lifted her head till her mouth was inches from his. 'Yes?' she murmured invitingly.

And, just as his frown deepened, she heard a wail.

His hands dropped away abruptly. 'Perfect timing,' he drawled.

Her eyes narrowed. What did he mean by that? Shaking, she began to stride across the room to the kitchen. Did he think that the interruption meant that he could successfully evade her questions?

Or…that he'd been saved the bother of rejecting her unwanted advances? She went hot with embarrassment.

How could she have been so stupid? Yes, she could hardly breathe for the ache of physical emptiness. Yes, she wanted Blake to make love to her. Badly. But that didn't mean she had to bat her lashes at him like a besotted schoolgirl!

It was all that talk of behaving like a flower child, she

thought with a rueful sigh, and hurried into the kitchen to console herself with cuddling her baby. 'Hey, sweetheart! You're hungry again, aren't you?' she murmured fondly, weakly smiling her thanks as she took Luc from Mrs Carter's soothing, sudsy arms.

'Now, you shouldn't be dashing in to him the minute he cries,' the cook chided amiably. 'Poor lamb. You look quite pale. Shall I do you a cocoa?'

'I'll see to Nicole,' came a low growl from behind her.

Nicole tensed as Blake came in to dominate the room. Her skin burned. The atmosphere seemed to thicken and she even looked up from under her lashes to see if the cook had sensed it and was puzzled. But Mrs Carter was busily stacking plates as if the electrical charge in the air didn't exist.

'I can manage,' Nicole jerked out. 'Honestly, I don't need anyone—'

'Why don't you pack up for the night, Mrs Carter?' Blake suggested, ignoring Nicole's babbling. 'You've done more than enough for us. Maisie can clear away the rest of the things in the morning.' He put his hand on the cook's broad shoulder. 'You did us proud. Dinner was superb,' he said more gently. 'Thank you for all your trouble. Goodnight, then. Sleep well.'

'If you're sure…'

'Positive.'

Nicole's heart sank as Mrs Carter rinsed and dried her fingers then trundled heavily out to a chorus of goodnights. Now Blake would read the riot act, Nicole thought glumly. Accuse her of low morals. Declare that any woman who offered herself to a virtual stranger must have come from a sexually liberal household…

'Your child is crying.'

Her huge eyes swivelled to Blake's. 'Do you think I don't know that?' she flared. 'I'm waiting for you to go!'

He studied her coolly, never taking those piercing, coal-black eyes from hers. And all her body was melting—bone, flesh, sinew, while her blood surged and raged till every cell felt energised and frighteningly alive.

This wasn't good for Luc. She must calm down. But she couldn't, not while Blake remained in the same room, pushing out all that testosterone at her.

His eyes seemed drowsy. Sternly, she told herself he was tired.

'Do you want cocoa?'

The banal words were spoken in a husky undertone that caused turmoil within her. She sat down quickly with her back to him.

'No!' she grated. 'Just get out!'

His hand touched her shoulder and she jumped. His fingers idly pushed her shoulder strap to and fro. For a moment she thought he was going to slide it down to reveal her breast. She felt every inch of her body tingle in anticipation and she willed him to do it, even though she knew it would be the act of a man who thought she was a slut.

'Goodnight,' he muttered in hard, crisp tones and left.

The door banged shut. Trembling, she eased off the strap, intensely aware of the burning imprint of his fingers still branding her skin as if he'd claimed her for his undisputed possession.

'Oh, Luc! My little sweetheart,' she whispered in despair as she settled him for his feed. 'I've made such a mistake. He despises me. I've failed your grandfather.'

She leaned back in the chair until the tumult of her thoughts grew less frantic. Gazing down at her son, she reflected that he was the most important thing in her life. He would not grow up with the spectre of a wronged grandfather hanging over his head. She could never rest while people were thinking such awful things about her father. It pained her. She couldn't bear injustice.

In the morning she would ask her own questions. There would be plenty of people around who'd remember Giles Bellamie. To hell with washing her dirty linen in public! She wouldn't be beaten by Blake's refusal to consider he might be mistaken.

Maybe she'd never gain his respect where she was concerned. But she'd force him to grovel and admit he was wrong about her father. She must, for Luc's sake.

Six o'clock. Silently, she packed her case and got Luc ready for the day. He didn't seem hungry and was unusually grizzly, so it took her a while before he was dressed in his little blue romper suit.

But that morning she felt she could cope with anything. Despite her mind teeming with thoughts, she'd had a good night. It wasn't surprising since the day before had been exhausting. Seemingly a lifetime had been lived in just twenty-four hours.

Refreshed, she slipped on one of her favourite flowing summer skirts and a cropped top then tidied the room so Mrs Carter or Maisie wouldn't have to do too much once she'd gone.

Her pre-breakfast playtime with Luc was briefer than usual. Just a few cuddles, a tickle of his round tummy and some kisses and words of love. 'Things to do,' she murmured, nuzzling his little pink toes. 'People to see, reputations to uphold. Come on, sweetheart. You wait here in your crib while I get things organised.'

She started up the musical mobile which Mrs Carter had attached to the crib and for a moment Luc stopped grizzling, his huge blue eyes fixed in wonder on the whirling musical farmyard.

Hoping there were no burglar alarms, and steeling herself for the sound of screaming sirens just in case, she tiptoed down the stairs and left her case in a corner of the hall. Then she returned for Luc, who seemed to be fretting again. 'Hush, sweetheart, hush. Mummy's here now. She's going to have breakfast—' she whispered into his miniature ear as she hurried down towards the kitchen '—and then we'll explore the village. All right?' She deposited a kiss on the screwed-up nose and he stopped whimpering for a moment. 'After that, we'll have an early coffee and then get rooms somewhere—*oh*!'

In the doorway she stopped in confusion. A tousle-haired, unshaven and bleary-eyed Blake was sitting at the kitchen table and scowling at her over a bone china mug of steaming coffee. He looked so disheveled and disreputable and utterly gorgeous in tight black jeans and the torso-embracing T-shirt that she was lost for words. And her heart was thumping crazily. All her embarrassment of the previous night was forgotten. This Blake was dangerous—almost feral. With an animal quality that made her shiver with fear and excitement at the same time.

'You!' he growled ungraciously.

She gulped at his hostility. But wouldn't be cowed. Maybe in his eyes she was cheap, but he had no right to be rude to a guest in his house. She'd made a mistake. Read the signs wrongly. Did that make her so contemptible? Men made passes without being labelled as tarts!

'Me.' Her chin lifted in defiance. 'Why so surprised?'

'You're up early,' he complained and looked as if he might lock her up for such a crime.

Nicole boldly marched in. 'You didn't mention there was a curfew,' she said sarcastically. 'I must remind Luc not to wake up till eight if I'm ever in this house again.'

That should shut him up! Head high, she stalked over to the kettle and carried it to the tap, intending to juggle the grizzling Luc in one arm and prepare her breakfast with one hand and the occasional use of an elbow, as mothers had probably done for centuries.

The kettle was tugged from her grip. 'See to him.' He wrenched open the tap. 'I'll make you some tea.'

It sounded as if he'd prefer it to be arsenic and strychnine combined. She glared. 'I was going to cook something—'

'I'll do it.'

'I'd prefer to do it myself,' she retorted, 'than have you curdling the eggs with your bad temper.'

'Luc needs you. He's not settled. Give your attention to him and let me do your breakfast then you can both get out of this house and be on your way.'

Grumpily, Blake aimed the plug at the socket and pushed it in then snapped on the switch. She watched him stomp over to the fridge and grab bacon, eggs and sausages. If he wanted to be a martyr, then let him.

'A tomato would be nice, too,' she commented perkily.

He scowled and she giggled. 'Glad it's amusing,' he muttered.

She paused in trying to cheer Luc up and laughed. 'You just look so cross! Are you always such a grouch in the mornings?'

'Are you always so darn cheerful?' he countered.

She made a face. 'I don't have much choice. Luc is usually ready for fun and games by the time the sun rises. Hey,' she said to her son. 'This grumpiness is catching! Where's your happy face? Look. Here are the little piggies, one goes to market, one stays home…'

'When are you off?'

'Immediately after breakfast.' She saw him cover up a yawn. Noticed how slow his movements were. And put two and two together. 'Have you been out all night?' she enquired caustically, remembering his sarcastic references to her father's supposed excesses. 'Spent the night partying, have you?' And wondered with a sudden vicious spurt of jealousy who'd kept him up, who'd exhausted him, who'd put him in such a bad mood.

'Walking.' Expertly, he turned the sausages, scowling at them so hard she thought they might be horribly charred from his glare alone.

'In the dark?' she asked, intrigued and relieved that he hadn't been with a woman. Stupid. *Stupid!* she told herself.

'Full moon.'

'Hmm. You don't have any Transylvanian blood, do you?' she asked, her eyes big and innocent, her lashes batting up and down like mad.

He crushed her merriment with one scornful glance. 'If I were a vampire,' he said tightly, 'I'd have claimed you last night.' Avoiding her wide-eyed look as she coped with the wicked thrill that curled through her veins, he raked through his already mussed-up hair then massaged his temples as if they hurt. 'Why don't you amuse your child and leave me in peace?'

'Oh,' she said with exaggerated understanding. 'Hangover!'

He slammed a knife and fork on the table, then the salt and pepper were similarly tested to destruction.

'Not on two whiskies,' he growled.

'So there's no excuse for your bad temper,' she countered in a flash.

His breath sheared in. 'I have reasons.' It seemed that his eyes glittered with anger. 'You're definitely one of them.'

'Oh!' She felt crushed.

There was a silence, broken only by the sizzling food in the pan and her increasingly desperate attempts to make Luc smile. Suddenly a plate was banged in front of her.

'Give him to me while you eat.'

'No, thanks. He's not too happy today and...' Her voice

died away. Blake had thrust his face very close to hers and she could see he was explosively angry.

'I want you to leave as soon as possible,' he said through his teeth. 'If you hang on to Luc then I'll be forced to cut up your food for you and feed it to you, mouthful by mouthful. Is that what you want?'

The image of being fed by Blake was inescapably erotic. Her heart began to pound as if it might leap from her body. There was passion in his face and a wild, almost uncontrolled blaze in his eyes. She almost said yes. That was what she wanted.

Gulping, she pushed Luc at him and Blake was forced to move back. She felt as if she'd come up for air after being half-drowned.

With trembling fingers she picked up her knife and fork and went through the motions of eating. She pushed food into her mouth—but only because he'd realise how disturbed she'd been by his threat if she left it untouched.

After a moment she had recovered her composure a little. Enough to notice Blake lightly tossing Luc in the air. Her son betrayed her totally by squealing with laughter and thoroughly enjoying every stomach-swooping second.

While she scurried through her meal they went on to more delights. Like 'see how near the ceiling you can get' and 'whirl around like a pancake' games. Blake's enjoyment of her son—and Luc's joyous surrender to the rough and tumble of inescapably exciting male bonding activities—made her blurt out, 'I am going. But I'm staying in the village, you know.'

The pancake spun to a sudden halt and looked rather surprised. Blake looked as if he'd been told she ate babies for lunch. 'I don't think so!' he hissed, tucking Luc over his shoulder in an infuriatingly expert way.

'I have some enquiries to make,' she said smugly, tackling the last piece of bacon with great satisfaction.

He studied her thoughtfully. 'No one will accommodate you.'

She shot him a suspicious glance. 'Because you're Mr Big around here?'

'Something like that,' he replied laconically.

Her jaw dropped open. 'Are you telling me that you'd order people not to give me bed and breakfast?' she cried in astonishment.

'If necessary.'

'But that's...that's...'

'Unfair use of authority.'

He didn't seem at all bothered by that. On the contrary, he seemed positively proud of his intended behaviour.

'Why?' she demanded.

'Simple. I don't want you pestering people just because you can't accept that your father was—'

'Don't say it!' she yelled, leaping to her feet. 'You may make everyone here dance like puppets on a string, but somehow I'll discover the truth! There are other villages nearby. Other pubs to stay in. Give me my son. I want to get out of this house.' She took Luc from him and felt unbelievably upset when her baby began to grizzle again. 'I'll be back with evidence, Blake Bellamie, and then you'll apologise to me on your bended knees!' she snapped.

'On my knees to you?' he queried, his eyes hotly dark and lustrous. And she was instantly alight with a terrible sexual hunger. He smiled speculatively. 'Forgive me if I don't hold my breath,' he drawled.

'Just you wait!' she muttered, furious with herself for responding so eagerly every time he put on that sexy look. Hair bouncing angrily, she spun on her heel and stormed to the door.

'Just a minute!' he commanded.

'What now?' she asked, turning to face him defiantly.

'Something you forgot,' he growled and she felt a *frisson* of danger rip through her body.

'What?' she mouthed.

She knew what he was going to do but she couldn't move, couldn't stop him. Their gazes clashed. His was black and pouring out hungry fires that seared her flesh and made it burn. Her parched lips parted as she struggled for breath, hope and fear tangling in her mind and a wild need destroying her urge to turn tail and run.

In seconds he had closed the gap between them, his closeness almost suffocating her. Before she could move a muscle he had caught her shoulders and his mouth had come down hard on hers in a hard, thorough and intensely erotic kiss that made her moan with desperate longing.

Only seconds later he stepped back, his expression utterly non-committal. She couldn't breathe at all. Her mouth felt hot. As if it had been abandoned. Wide-eyed, she stared at him in bewilderment.

'Why…what…?' she choked out.

'I believe you were expecting that last night,' he said scathingly, his body and face rigid with tightly controlled emotions.

It was true, of course. That made it worse. Her skin turned to flame. 'I—I don't understand—' she stumbled.

'Just to let you know that things happen only when I want them to. I call the shots around here—'

'Oh, Mr Very Big indeed!' she flung.

'That's right.' His eyes darkened. 'A warning, Nicole,' he added with soft menace. 'Set one foot on my land or pester people in the village, and I will broadcast your father's misdemeanours, even if it means shaming my family name.'

'You mean…?' She gulped. 'No one knows about this rumour that he was wicked?'

'Of course not. It was a private family matter,' he answered curtly. 'But make no mistake about it, if you pursue this matter then I'll drag his reputation into the mud. Contrary to what you might think, I don't rule here as a tyrant. I am respected. My word is unquestioned. So, if you know what's good for you—and your father's memory—get out of Great Aston and don't come back until you're invited. Or you'll find yourself in a hell of your own making.'

CHAPTER SEVEN

'HELLO, Daddy! Hello, Nicole, hello, baby!'

They both jumped as the irrepressible figure of Josef came leaping in, dressed in a Monsterman outfit over his school clothes.

'Oh, dear,' he muttered, skidding to a halt and looking from one tense face to the other. 'You're having a row. Shall I go out and come back in again so you can pretend everything's all right?'

In that split second Nicole knew that he must have witnessed his mother arguing with Blake. And that the perceptive child had probably slipped quietly away until a false polite atmosphere was restored. Her heart went out to him and she was desperately thinking of a way to reassure him when Blake spoke.

'What,' he asked with frightening self-control, 'are you doing up at this time?'

'I woke up and went into your bedroom and your bed hadn't been slept in. So I got dressed and went to see Granny and told her all that, but she didn't know where you were either.' Josef beamed at his father. 'I said a pretty lady had stayed here last night and she raised her eyebrow like you do. Did you sleep in Nicole's bed, Daddy?'

'No!' he and Nicole shouted in unison.

Josef jumped back, startled, his lower lip trembling. 'What did I say?' he complained. 'Granny said, "Aah, so that's it!" as if you *had*. And she asked me to bring her some orange juice and tell her more about—'

'I'll do that,' Blake muttered, striding to the fridge. He poured juice into a glass.

'So you weren't arguing 'cos you took all the duvet and left Nicole cold, Dad?'

Blake's mouth tightened. 'No! You get yourself some breakfast.' He made for the door. 'I'll be back in a moment,' he muttered, and disappeared.

Nursing the fretful Luc, Nicole smiled consolingly at an unusually subdued Josef. 'Your Daddy and I have only just met,' she said gently. 'It's usually only married people who share a bed—'

'Debbie Barker's not married to Pete's Dad and they sleep together,' announced Josef, pouring cereal into a bowl.

Nicole sighed. You couldn't fudge things with children. 'I expect they know each other very well, though,' she suggested.

'Oh, ever so. Pete says they have baths together. Will you and Daddy do that when you're proper friends?'

'I prefer showers,' Nicole said faintly.

'There's room for two in Daddy's,' Josef informed her helpfully. 'But you couldn't play with Monsterman slides or motor boats or anything like that.'

'I think,' Nicole said hastily, behaving like an abject coward and avoiding any further comment, 'that Luc needs changing. Excuse us a moment.'

Hurrying over to the sofa, she laid out the changing mat and placed the wailing Luc on it.

'I told Granny you were nicer than any of Daddy's lady friends,' the irrepressible Josef announced through a mouthful of cereal.

'That's very flattering. Thank you,' she said, wondering how many 'lady friends' the little boy had endured. Probably dozens, she thought, judging by Blake's testosterone levels. Did they all coo over Josef or had they found his frank outspoken manner disconcerting? Granny clearly knew what the arrival of a female meant in this house. Blake must be something of a womaniser.

'I didn't know you had a granny here,' she said idly.

'She's in bed all the time. I only get to see her once a day with Dad. I think she's got leg trouble. Maisie said she was on her last legs, anyway.'

'Oh! I'm so sorry,' Nicole cried, her face falling in dismay. Poor Blake, she thought. It must be hard for him with his mother so ill.

Her mind was occupied with this as she was unbuttoning the little romper suit. It was a moment before she realised to her horror that Luc's skin was covered in a rash that hadn't been there earlier. With shaking hands she quickly changed her son and, in as level a tone as she could manage, she called out to Josef, 'Would you bring a glass tumbler to me, please?'

'Does he drink orange juice too?' the little boy asked with interest, meandering over with nail-biting slowness.

'No!'

In panic, Nicole snatched the glass from him and pressed it against Luc's skin to test for meningitis. The rash disappeared. She sank back on her haunches in relief. The glass dropped from her nerveless fingers and was caught by a large, tanned hand.

'Trouble?' Blake asked urgently.

She put her hand to her forehead, trying to compose herself but she was shaking dreadfully. After a moment, Blake's arm came around her.

'Take it slowly. Breathe deeply,' he rasped. 'That rash—'

'It's not meningitis!' she whispered, burying her head in Blake's accommodating shoulder. He was probably annoyed with her for being so bold, but she needed comfort and he was the only person available. 'It's something else—but it's not that!' She raised a tragic face. 'Oh, Blake! I thought... I thought...'

'OK, OK.'

When she continued to shake, he hesitated for a moment and then with a half-suppressed sigh he hugged her tightly, his arms wrapping around her securely. She inhaled the musky maleness of him, felt the firmness of his warm body, and was instantly reassured.

Then a little hand inserted itself into hers too, and she pulled away to see Josef's small, anxious face.

'It's all right,' she said jerkily, calming herself for the child's sake. She found a weak smile because his lower lip was trembling, and squeezed Josef's little hand. 'I thought Luc might be very ill but it's probably nothing dreadful at all.'

Blake released her, leapt to his feet and moved swiftly over to the phone, saying with measured authority that brooked no refusal, 'But we'll get the doctor round, just to be sure. Joe, finish your cereal, make some toast and get yourself ready for school. Susie will take you this morning. You'll find her in the stables. All right?'

'Yes, Dad. Will do. If—if anything's wrong, will you—?'

'I'll ring the school either way. Promise. Good lad.' Blake gave his son an approving nod and began to speak in low, urgent tones into the phone.

Nicole's heart was pumping hard. Sinking to the comfort of the sofa, she cradled her beloved son, praying that the rash wasn't serious. It could have so many causes—and she couldn't bear Luc to be in danger. He was her whole life now. She had to keep him safe. She'd do anything, *anything* to protect him. Her lip trembled and she felt alarmingly close to tears.

'He'll be here in a few minutes. Hey. Don't worry,' Blake said when she raised blurred eyes to his. 'Everything will be fine.' He came to sit beside her and surprised her by taking her shaking hand in his.

She looked up at him gratefully. 'Thank you,' she whispered. 'I—I can cope with almost anything, but the thought of—of…' She couldn't say it. Her father's death had been hard enough to bear, but the idea that her little baby might… 'I'm sorry!' she gulped, choking back the tears.

A handkerchief dabbed at her eyes. His face was very close and it seemed less angry than before. Warmer. Kinder.

'It's all right to be upset. I understand,' he said in a gravelly voice. 'I felt exactly the same helplessness when Josef had gastroenteritis once.'

'I remember,' chirped in Josef. 'I was mega-sick everywhere. Dad kept clearing it up. Yuk! And that's not all. I had the most awful—'

'Do your toast, Joe, and save us from the less pleasant details,' Blake said drily. He turned back to Nicole, who gave him a sympathetic roll of her eyes at Josef's lack of delicacy. His finger lightly touched her wryly smiling mouth and she held her breath. 'Embarrassing he might be,' Blake murmured, 'but he's made you smile.'

She mastered her racing pulses. 'He'd make a slab of stone smile,' she said ruefully.

'I deserve a reward, don't I? Can I ride my pony to school, Dad?' Josef asked, clearly taking advantage of this highly satisfactory praise.

'No. You walk like everyone else. And don't reel off a list of children who come by car. You know what I mean.'

Josef closed his open mouth and Nicole smiled again, seeing that Blake had guessed right. Then the little boy perked up and adopted another tack. 'Will Nicole and Luc be here when I get back?' he asked hopefully.

Blake let out a long hiss of breath that managed to sound resigned and irritated at the same time. 'Probably.'

'Good. I can show them my beetles.'

'Depending on how Luc is,' Blake warned. 'He might not be up to beetles.'

She couldn't read anything into his tone but she knew he didn't welcome her enforced stay. He'd made his feelings about her clear enough last night, however kind he was being about Luc now. But he wasn't a monster. His sympathy lay purely with her baby, not with her, so she needn't kid herself that he'd had a change of heart.

'I'm very sorry about this,' she said awkwardly. 'I really was intending to leave—'

He grunted. 'Now you can't,' he said and she still wasn't sure from the low growl if he was annoyed or reluctantly accepting that fact. 'I can hardly turn you out with a sick baby, can I?'

'Blake…'

She hesitated. More than anything she wanted to assure him that she respected and admired him. And as a consequence she wanted to make discreet enquiries to clear her father's name. Deep down, she longed to be accepted by him as a member of the family. For a relationship to build up between them all—Blake, Josef, Luc and herself. He was her kinsman. The only family she had, other than Luc.

How could she say what was in her heart? But then, what did she have to lose?

Blake was perplexed. It felt so right, holding her hand, protecting her, trying to ease her worries. He didn't understand why, only that his entire being was rebelling against his decision to keep her away from Cranford at all costs. Something told him that she had qualities he might appreciate and value. She'd consistently been thoughtful towards his son and she was a devoted mother. He frowned. Only a short time ago, when he'd taken up the glass of orange juice, his mother had expressed a hope that he'd met 'a nice girl' at last.

He'd smiled wryly and assured her that he hadn't indulged in a night of passion and that his appearance was due to a lack of sleep after badger-watching in Sawpit meadow rather than romping all night in a nubile girlfriend's bed.

'Shame,' she'd said, surprising him. 'Be happy, my darling,' she'd urged. 'Go with your heart and your gut instincts. Don't make my mistake.'

Tactfully, ruefully, checking his retort that it was she who'd taught him to suppress his feelings, he'd kissed her, promising to read to her before lunch and to tell her a little about Nicole. Though how much he'd reveal he wasn't sure yet.

And now his heart and his guts were telling him to give Nicole a chance. To let her stay and to see if she could be trusted with Cranford.

'You were about to say something,' he murmured.

'It's nothing,' she said.

'It's troubling you. I can see that by your frown.' Again he had to touch her. The faint V between her brows. She lowered her lashes and bit her lip. 'Why don't you say what you want to?' he suggested, his heart and guts churning at the tenderness of her expression as she rocked and kissed her tiny baby.

He felt her take a deep breath. 'When the doctor's been,' she said. 'I can't think straight before that.'

'Of course.'

There was the sound of crunching close by. Blake looked up to see a worried Josef munching on a partially burnt piece of toast.

'He'll be all right, won't he, Dad?'

Disregarding the shower of sooty crumbs, Blake pulled his worried son on to his knee and gave him a cuddle. 'We have the best doctor in the Cotswolds. Of course he'll be all right. Now. Got everything you need?'

'PE kit, lunch money, hanky, string, Monsterman swaps, banana, chocolate bar, owl's pellets, lucky stone, empty matchbox, strip of leather and magpie feathers,' Josef replied in a solemn chant.

Nicole looked at Blake questioningly. 'Don't ask,' he muttered and slid from the sofa, taking his son with him. After a chorus of goodbyes and hugs, he managed to push Josef through the door just as Steve ushered himself in.

'Morning, Blake! Is that the patient over there? Blond as a Bellamie, isn't he? Morning, young lady. I'm Dr Steve Mackenzie. Let's have a look at the little man while Blake makes me some tea, shall we?'

Blake took one look at Nicole's white, frightened face and at that moment he would have done anything to stop her worrying. He was astonished. He cared about her. Why the devil was that? Perhaps his capacity for human sympathy was greater than he'd imagined. Perhaps he'd feel like this about any woman whose baby was ill. He dismissed his doubts as to the truth of that and focused on making Steve a mug of tea.

But he couldn't stop his heart thudding like crazy as the doctor examined little Luc and very gently asked a battery of searching questions.

Silent and restraining his urge to yell at Steve to make a diagnosis and put Nicole out of her misery, Blake placed the incongruous Monsterman mug on a side table beside Steve.

'Well, Nicole,' he said eventually and Blake found himself leaning forward for the verdict.

Steve flashed a reassuring smile at her and she looked slightly less anxious. At that moment, Blake wanted to catch her in his arms and shield her from the troubles of the world. Hell. He was going mad.

'What is it?' he demanded, far more abruptly than was proper.

Steve blinked his surprise then turned back to Nicole.

'Probably nothing to worry about—'

'Oh! *Grâce à Dieu!*' she said huskily, snuggling her face into Luc's small body.

Blake's throat developed a huge lump of emotion inside it. 'He's not in any danger?' he grated. He felt Nicole's eyes on him. Knew she was thinking that now she'd be thrown out. And so he smiled at her in reassurance.

Steve coughed for attention and they both gave a little jump. Blake could see his friend was wondering what was going on between them. Their gazes had held for a fraction too long.

Briskly he said, 'OK, Steve. Let's hear it.'

Looking slightly amused, the doctor turned his attention to Nicole again. 'You're doing all the right things. You're breast-feeding so that rules out many contagious diseases because that protects Luc from them. I reckon he's had an allergic reaction, perhaps to the crab you had last night—so don't eat any more shellfish, just in case.'

'I caused this?' she cried in horror.

'Don't beat yourself up,' advised Steve with a genial smile. 'You've tested his immune system and given yourself a bit of a shock, nothing more. If you want punishment, I imagine you've had enough in the past ten minutes or so.'

'You're right!' she muttered. 'I died a thousand deaths in a split second.'

'Then relax. Things will only get better. Keep him cool. I'll call in later to see how he's doing but ring me if he seems feverish or any worse—though I don't think this'll be the case. No aspirin for him or you…'

Blake listened to the instructions and felt a wash of relief flood through him. And, to be honest, a small surge of elation. Totally against his better judgement, Nicole was being forced to stay in the house. And to his amazement he felt overjoyed.

Steve waved a cheerful goodbye, extracted a promise of a game of tennis later that week, gave him a conspiratorial wink that was entirely superfluous and they were alone again.

Blake went over to her immediately, drawn by the fragile vulnerability of her drawn face. 'It's good news,' he said, his stiff tone at odds with his joyous feelings.

'Yes.' There was a long pause. She stared miserably at Luc, who seemed more settled. 'I could... I should be able to leave when the doctor's been this afternoon.'

'I don't think so.'

He saw her swallowing. When her huge, wet-lashed eyes lifted to his he felt a kick of tenderness ripping through him, as fierce as any anger.

'But you don't want me here,' she said in a low voice.

How could he answer that? With the truth—that he did want her around but couldn't trust himself not to keep his hands off her? And that he feared the release of the volcanic passions he was storing up?

'Come into the garden,' he said. 'Luc's asleep. I'll fetch the baby buggy and you can sit in the shade beneath the cedar. You can tell me what you wanted to say.' He took a deep breath and decided to give her a chance. 'And I can explain why I've been so determined to get you out of the house as soon as possible.'

CHAPTER EIGHT

IMMEDIATELY she stepped outside a sensation of serenity stole over her. Despite the grandeur of her surroundings she felt at home. Maybe this was because she recognised so many of the trees and shrubs, but also because the garden had been designed to please the eye and was a clever combination of formality and apparent, but well-ordered, chaos.

Blake brought Luc's buggy and then carried over two hugely comfortable steamer chairs which looked as if they might be Edwardian. Nicole sank into the deep cream cushions and gazed around, enchanted.

The unrestricted view across the mirror-still waters of a large lake to the wooded hills beyond was quite breathtaking and she felt calmer just by sitting there and looking at the view.

Eventually she turned to Blake, grateful that he'd given her time to let the lovely garden bring peace to her troubled mind.

'What do you think of it?' he asked, watching her intently.

She smiled. 'That I've never seen anywhere more beautiful,' she answered with a quiet sigh and his consequent smile of delight was just dazzling.

'I've spent years changing it from the stark, formal avenues of yew and box favoured by my...father,' he confided, his voice ringing with justifiable pride after the odd but brief hesitation.

'You?' she cried in astonishment. 'But this is the work

of someone with an artist's eye. And a love and knowledge of plants—'

'When you take over a place like this you have a great responsibility to ensure that it survives in good heart.' He looked at her intently, as though it was important she knew that. 'Those who inherit historic land and estates are only trustees. It is a duty to preserve everything that is good and to make the land financially viable. I made it my business to learn about landscape design and the use of plants.' He smiled to himself. 'There's something about being outside, even in the worst weather—digging, planting, weeding and tending—that lifts my soul,' he said to her surprise.

And she detected an underlying passion, too, that conveyed his enthusiasm even more than his words. Sparkling with animation, his eyes devoured the riotous borders, the foaming blossom and much-loved plants.

'You love it very much, don't you?' she murmured.

'Every bit of it. It's my creation. Part of me. Like Cranford itself,' he said quietly.

'And does Josef feel the same?'

Blake frowned. 'Passionately. He helps. Whenever he's missing I know I'll find him in the garden doing something useful. He needs to be out in the open air, like me, engaged in a physical activity.'

'I wonder that you have the time to be hands-on, with the estate and that huge house to manage,' she mused.

'It's not easy but I have a good staff who've been with me for years. I pay them well and they love Cranford enough to take care of it. But I have little spare time, it's true. Of course,' he said, his tone changing oddly, 'I was brought up knowing I'd inherit. I followed my…father around the estate much as Josef follows me.' He looked away and she could only see his jaw but it was tense and she wondered why. 'My son would be lost if he had to leave this house. Absolutely devastated,' he said, almost with a tinge of harshness in his tone.

'I—I'm sure that's true,' she said, aware that he was on edge but not knowing why. Then a reason occurred to her. In dismay she cried, 'You're not thinking you might have to sell for financial reasons, are you?'

He gave a short, oddly mirthless laugh. 'My finances are in good heart. We were in debt when I took over but now the estate is profitable because I dared to make changes. Apart from the farm, there are estate cottages bringing in rent. I employ a blacksmith, a potter and a printer, all of whom make items for the tourist trade.'

'My goodness!' she murmured, impressed.

'That's not all. We have Pick Your Own soft fruit and a farm shop, lease fishing rights on the lake and river, and hold weddings and functions in the old orangerie. The diary is full. In fact,' he said, 'there's a conference taking place this afternoon.'

'Oh. Do you need to go off to organise it?' she asked, feeling a lurch of disappointment at the prospect of losing his company.

'My PA is doing that. But I'll put in an appearance to check everything and I'll wander over in the evening when the fireworks are let off.'

She gazed at him in frank admiration.

'You've probably saved the estate from being broken up.'

'I can't argue with that,' he agreed. 'It was in a bad state when I took over.'

'What an achievement,' she mused. 'It must make you feel good inside to know that it'll continue in your family for your descendants to enjoy. No wonder Josef is full of self-confidence. His future is utterly secure.'

She smiled, thinking how comforting it must be to be part of such an inheritance. Not for the financial security but the sense of belonging, of being part of a community. And she wished her background wasn't so complicated by secrets and diverging opinions.

'Nothing,' Blake said quietly, 'is ever secure.'

'Well, with all those activities providing income you're hardly going to lose Cranford Hall to some outsider!' She laughed at such a ridiculous idea. 'No one would run it as well as you clearly do, anyway. You and Josef are absolutely right for this place, I can see that.'

There was a long silence while Blake stared out at the view to his far right. Perturbed at the idea of talking to the back of his head, she lightly touched his arm. He flinched and she bit her lip. That wasn't the reaction she'd hoped for.

'Blake. Please. We are cousins. I want us to be… friends.'

That was untrue. She wanted more. Heaving a deep sigh, she plucked up all her courage and continued. Her father had always told her to face up to mistakes and to see yourself as honestly as possible, warts and all. It was time she apologised for batting her eyes at him the previous evening.

'I know what you thought of me last night,' she ventured bravely.

'I doubt it,' he drawled.

She bit her lip. He wasn't making it easy for her. Fair enough. He didn't like being propositioned by women he didn't fancy.

'OK. I'll level with you. I was encouraging you because I find you very attractive. If I embarrassed you then I'm sorry. I've never behaved like that before in the whole of my life.' She gave a small, deprecating laugh. 'I'm totally inexperienced, to be honest. My ex-husband, Jean-Paul, was my only lover, the only man who's ever kissed me till…till…'

'Till I did.'

He turned his head and for a moment his eyes lingered on her mouth, making it tingle. She swallowed and resisted the urge to lick her lips. Too much of an invitation, even though she wanted to feel his mouth on hers again. She gave an inward groan as he jerked his head away again. How shameless she was!

'Yes. I—I don't know what happened to me last night. Perhaps the emotions of the day... I have no explanation, only that I wanted to be kissed by you. It was an impulse that I regret. Since you have no interest in me, it won't happen again.'

He turned to her then. 'Won't it?' he asked with a frown.

Reaching out, he stroked her cheek but was still frowning as he did so and she wondered if he was testing her. Even so, she quivered and marvelled at the power of his touch to arouse her. She gritted her teeth and forced herself to concentrate hard on what she wanted to say because it was so important that she cleared the air of any misunderstanding.

'I can take a hint. You made your feelings clear. Blake, I want you to forget what happened,' she went on doggedly. 'I am used to expressing my feelings and I can see that I must have seemed pushy and...' She remembered one of her father's favourite words, usually used to describe scantily dressed celebrities who flaunted their attributes in public. 'I was brazen, I know, and I apologise. Please forgive me!' she begged. 'We got on so well before you knew who I was. It was fun talking to you during dinner, too, after Josef broke the ice between us. If you block me out of your life, I have no family other than Luc.'

Eager to plead her cause, she leaned forward, her eyes beseeching him. 'You can't turn your back on us. There's been a misunderstanding about my father and I think we can sort it out, given time.' She held out her hand, her gaze steady and level on his dark, unfathomable eyes. 'Be my family. Be my cousin, for our children's sakes,' she begged.

It was a risk, he thought. But one he desperately wanted to take. Both honour and instinct were urging him to give her this chance to prove her father's innocence. And he knew he would forever regret it if he sent her away without searching for the truth.

There was something extraordinarily dignified about her manner. He thought of the way she'd responded to Josef and of the adoration in her eyes whenever she looked at her baby or touched him. There was a goodness in her, he felt sure.

Besides, she was a Bellamie and he couldn't turn his back on her. Wryly he acknowledged that his life had become confusing and unpredictable where it had once been stable and uneventful. Not long ago he'd known what the morrow would bring. But with Nicole around life had suddenly changed. One day he was threatening her, the next saw him welcoming her into his home.

It was the baby's illness, of course—that had forced his hand. And while Luc and Nicole waited under the protection of his roof—how could he do otherwise?—it did make sense to make some enquiries about Giles. And to find out more about Nicole.

Yes. He was acting sensibly. Couldn't reproach himself for changing his mind. And as if knowing he'd capitulated, his pulses leapt with an almost uncontainable excitement that swept through his body with a force he could not deny. He knew that all his logical reasons for letting her stay were as nothing compared with his need for her. To make love to her. Possess that body. Touch her, breathe in the scent of her, sate himself until the destructive hunger abated and he could think clearly again.

Nicole watched the changing expressions on his face

with apprehension. He stared at her for a long, breathless moment.

Then, to her delight, he took her hand in his. There was a new warm liquidity to his eyes and she felt dizzy with hope and longing.

'Cousin,' he said huskily. 'How could I resist such an impassioned plea?'

'Uhuh,' she managed, her lips parting as she fought breathlessness.

'I think we might be...*kissing* cousins,' he whispered.

She was astonished. Slowly, as his face came closer and closer, her eyes began to close. The anticipation was sweetly painful.

But the moment his mouth touched hers she felt something inside her snap. With a groan she caught his strong face between her hands and deepened the kiss till her senses reeled from the onslaught of his hard, demanding mouth.

She found herself being drawn on to his lap. Passionate kisses rained on her face and throat even as she struggled to grasp the fact that he had wanted her after all. She felt wonderfully wanton and desirable. With a featherlight movement his hands had slid to the warm nakedness of her back between the hem of her cropped top and her skirt and she arched against him with a small moan of pleasure.

Then, reluctantly, she gently pushed against his chest and was released.

'Because of Luc,' she explained, panting heavily.

'Of course.'

She slid from his lap and sat shakily on her chair. Her mouth felt as if it had been brought to life. And unbelievably smiley. Her shining eyes met his and she didn't know how she didn't ravish him then and there, her need was so strong and his magnetism so incredibly powerful.

'I—I can't...while he...'

'I know,' he whispered. And his eyes promised 'later'. She felt a thrill electrify her entire body. Later. *Later!*

In her wildest dreams she'd never thought… She gave a slow, sexy smile and rejoiced when he clenched his teeth and tensed up in an effort not to reach out for her again. He did want her!

It seemed the fireworks had already begun. Something was certainly rocketing through her. A kind of wild joy, a hope and a growing certainty that their relationship would be very special. Perhaps even someone she could love. Her head whirled. Even from the very beginning she'd known there was an extraordinary chemistry between them. A bond, fiercer and even more urgent than blood itself. That was why she'd been confused by his rejection of her. In her bones, despite his apparent indifference, she'd had a suspicion that she'd been responding to the signals his body was sending out. The chemistry had been two-way. In future she'd listen to her instincts, she promised herself!

It quite shocked her that she could hardly keep her hands off him. At the same time it excited her that he felt the same, however hard he tried to hide it. She wanted to know, to feel, and to be the reason and an essential part of the passion that simmered beneath his restraint. Felt a wicked urge to be the one who drove him crazy till he forgot everything except making love to her.

She looked up at him from under her lashes, unknowingly alluring, unknowingly aping the seductive techniques of women out for all they could get.

Blake froze, remembering other women who'd thought to entice him into their power with their sexuality.

'Blake…you will let Luc and me stay for a while, won't you?' she breathed. 'I want to. So very much.'

It was an alluringly husky plea that came so close to her eager kisses and her sudden withdrawal. A trick he was well used to. His entire body tensed up.

Had she responded to him to get her own way? He felt sickened at the thought. He'd had enough of that from his ex-wife, who'd only agreed to have a child if she could profit financially. The memory of those months of cold-blooded bargaining chilled his ardour. He wouldn't be taken for a sucker again. Wouldn't be manipulated. Would never be a woman's victim again.

Nicole realised that he had withdrawn from her even though he had not actually moved. The closed look came into his eyes where once there had been glowing desire.

They were back to square one again.

'You don't trust me, do you?' she blurted out in dismay. 'You think I'll pervert Josef or the people here—'

'I don't know,' he muttered, pushing his hand through his hair till the black waves bounced in angry disorder. 'I'll level with you. I can't be sure about your motives for flirting with me—'

'My *motives?*' she flared. 'I don't have motives! I just *am*! Don't you think my behaviour might be something to do with sexual attraction?' she added indignantly.

He shrugged. 'You could be using sex to make me change my mind about you,' he said bluntly.

'Is that the kind of woman you're used to? A woman who sees her favours as a bargaining tool?' she asked in horror.

He gave a short laugh. 'Yes. I suppose I am.'

'Well, I'm sorry for you! But there are also women without...' She frowned. '*L'astuce.*'

'Guile.'

'That's right.' She made a mental note to ask him why he spoke French like a native. 'And women like that—like me—enjoy sex for what it is, not for what it can do for us.'

'Really,' he said in a husky croak.

'If I had any sense,' she said with a sigh, 'I'd behave

modestly and wear unrevealing clothes. Then you might question your belief that I've been brought up in a house of ill repute by a dissolute father.'

'So why—' he muttered, glaring as he angrily fingered her bare midriff and made her draw in her breath sharply '—are you doing exactly the opposite?'

Her eyes darkened. 'Because this is how I dress normally and…' She took a gamble. 'Where you're concerned, *and only you*, I can't help myself.'

From the startled look he gave her she knew he wanted to kiss her. That her honesty had rocked him. And it had also given him a free hand. Take me in your arms! she pleaded silently. Trust me.

She watched him struggling with his desires and her mouth parted in longing. When he tore his gaze from it and sat stubbornly back in his chair she felt a shaft of disappointment spear its way through her yearning body. She did so badly want him to like her as well as to lust after her.

'I have to remain objective about this,' he muttered. 'I can't just do as I please.' And added under his breath, 'So much is at stake.'

'I don't see the problem,' she argued. 'We're attracted to one another. We are free.'

'I want to stay free,' he growled.

Her face flushed. 'I'm not intending to behave like a nagging wife just because we make love! It's simple, Blake. We want one another. What's the big deal?'

'Are you always that frank about your feelings?' he asked.

He'd tried to sound cool and curious but his voice had shaken. At least, she thought, he does have the same urges—even if he's better at controlling them.

'Not about wanting someone. I've never felt this way before. I know women aren't supposed to be so…up front, but what am I supposed to do? Play coy and hard to get? I'm not like that, Blake. Everyone says I'm too open, though. I say what I feel. I don't believe in hiding my emotions, unless what I say or do might hurt someone,' she said quietly. 'My friends tell me I'm naive—childlike in my innocence and my inability to pretend.' She smiled, seeing that he had relaxed and his suspicious expression had vanished. 'Perhaps that's why I feel so close to Josef. He's refreshingly honest, isn't he?'

'To a fault,' Blake growled.

'But you don't correct him and make him into a social robot, do you?' she argued.

His brows drew hard together. 'No,' he said shortly. 'I had enough of that in my own childhood. My aim is to teach him to be kind and thoughtful and to put himself in other people's shoes.'

'Then we think alike. My father told me always to speak the truth and never to play games, especially with men.'

He rubbed his piratical five o'clock shadow. 'So you don't tell lies.'

'I'm hopeless at it! It's too complicated when you do!' she cried passionately. 'You have to remember what lies you told. It's far easier to be truthful.'

'Your husband.' Blake narrowed his eyes speculatively. 'Did he appreciate your honesty?'

She sighed. 'That was the problem.'

'Would you tell me why you broke up?'

'If it will help.'

'Possibly.'

With a flick of her finger she pushed back her hair behind her ears, her expression sad and reflective. 'OK. He wanted me to stay the same and never to get pregnant because that would change me from a wife into a mother.'

'He wanted your body to remain unchanged. Sexy and

unmarked by the ravages of motherhood,' Blake said quietly.

'Yes!' she cried in amazement. 'But how did you know?'

'My ex-wife was worried about her figure,' he said, his expression bitter.

'But,' argued Nicole, 'she did choose to be a mother. She had Josef—'

'Only because I promised her a hefty chunk of my fortune,' he muttered.

Nicole's eyes rounded in shock. 'That's awful!'

Blake gave a small shrug. 'I should never have agreed to such blatant blackmail. But I was trying to keep my marriage together. I thought that when Josef was born she'd be different, she'd love her child and would welcome motherhood.'

'But she didn't,' Nicole said with gentle sympathy.

His eyes darkened. 'She wouldn't even look at him. And I could never forgive her for neglecting her own flesh and blood. She stayed because she enjoyed her position here as lady of the manor. But she tired even of that. And she knew everyone in Great Aston disliked her for rejecting Josef. So, seeing that she wasn't going to get anything more from me, she left when he was almost three years old.'

'Is she happy, do you know, with the chauffeur?' Nicole asked tentatively.

'I've no idea. She hasn't even sent birthday cards to Joe.'

Nicole stared at him in horror.

'I can't understand that,' she said slowly.

Blake gave another perfunctory shrug. 'Some people think only of their own good. Their own needs. Their lives are dedicated to pleasing themselves and they are incapable of generosity or sacrifice for others.'

'I'm sorry you had that experience,' she said fervently.

'My fault. I was warned that my money and position would attract the wrong kind of woman.'

'But you loved her,' she said with understanding.

'I don't think so,' he said, surprising her. 'She was beautiful and lively and charmed her way around the social circuit. I mistook that for a loving nature. She's not wicked, Nicole. Just too immature to cope with anyone's needs but her own.'

She sighed. 'I can understand why you're wary of my motives. It's difficult to trust people after an experience like that. I suppose day after day you had to handle the fact that your wife was trying to manipulate you. But you have to risk trusting people, Blake, or you spend your whole life missing all the good, honest friendships you can make.'

He shook his head. 'I prefer that to being hurt again.'

'I'd rather be hurt than live like a hermit without someone to love, someone to give your heart to!' she declared.

He looked pained. Haunted.

'Let's get back to your own marriage,' he said, deftly changing the subject. 'You obviously became pregnant. I gather your husband didn't like that situation.'

'Worse than that. He was furious,' she confessed. 'Luc wasn't planned, you see.'

'You didn't want him?' he cried, aghast.

'Oh, yes!' she cried, clasping her hands in a passionate gesture. 'I *longed* to have a child! I was overjoyed when I knew I was pregnant. It seemed to complete my life.' She smiled lovingly with a long, lingering glance at her sleeping child and then her face grew sad again. 'I'm afraid Jean-Paul never forgave me. He stayed out late a lot. I told him I didn't like that in no uncertain terms. My friends said I should lure him back to me with intimate meals and sexy dresses that showed my cleavage.' She shrugged her slender shoulders. 'I felt that if he loved me he'd want to care for me and be with me.'

'A mature man would have coped with the changes to his life and yours,' Blake observed with contempt.

'Precisely. He was being selfish and just didn't love me enough. And, knowing that in my heart of hearts, I wasn't in any mood to put on an act and seduce him.'

'Presumably he had an affair.' Blake's gaze was very direct, very searching.

She wrinkled her nose in disgust. 'In our house, our bed, under my nose and with my best friend!'

'Doesn't get much worse than that!' he commented drily.

'Oh, it does, when you've caught him once, forgiven him and then find him and your friend in your bed again!' she muttered.

Blake frowned and swore.

'Yes,' she said bitterly. 'He was that and more. After the divorce he disappeared. He doesn't even know if he has a son or a daughter.'

He cursed again. 'So you've had no moral or financial support for Luc?'

'Oh, yes. From my father at first—'

'Just a minute.' His brows drew hard together. 'Luc's seven weeks old. Your father was alive till recently?'

She took a moment to speak, her eyes sad and haunted. The memories made her heart ache.

'Very much so. Dear Papa,' she mumbled to herself. 'He was so thrilled to be a grandfather. He'd sit and stare at Luc and smile as if he was the most precious thing on earth. And sometimes he'd be so moved that a little tear would drop to his cheek. I'd go to him and hug him and say he was going senile in his old age and…and he'd laugh and hold me tight and say he was happy for the first time since he was a young man. That shook me. I'd no idea he'd never been content with my mother.'

'Exactly when,' Blake murmured softly, 'did he die?'

The pain touched her eyes and drew down the corners of her mouth. 'A little over three weeks ago,' she whispered in a shaky voice.

He looked genuinely shocked. Her hands were gently caught in his. Compassion showed in his softened face and the sincerity of his sympathy brought tears to her eyes.

'I can't tell you how sorry I am. I've been hard on you. And you've been through hell,' he said huskily. He lifted her hands, one by one, and pressed a tender and deeply impassioned kiss on them.

'I loved him very much,' she choked. 'Miss him so badly.'

Blake's grip tightened but he didn't comment. His thumb lightly stroked the back of her hand while she struggled to push back the tears. She knew that she could never rest until Blake honoured her father's memory.

'How are you managing now?' he asked quietly.

'Papa had sold a couple of paintings and the buyer very kindly paid the money direct to me. I inherit his cottage so I have a home, and eventually there'll be his savings too when the executors have done their work. I can earn my living even while Luc's small because I can convert the piggery and put in an extractor fan for the glue fumes. Then I'll be able to repair and restore ceramics at home when Luc sleeps—either outside or in the house. I'm lucky, really. Luckier than most.'

'You have your future mapped out,' he said with a frown.

'I have Luc to think of. I must provide for him.'

'You are happy where you live in France?'

She wondered why he asked. Why he should care. Perhaps he was just being polite.

'I was,' she said honestly. 'But my father's death has changed everything. And I'm afraid that now I'm divorced my male friends think I'm fair game and my female friends are wary of me.'

'I can't blame them,' he said drily.

'But I'd never threaten their relationships!' she objected.

'You couldn't help it.'

'No! I'm not like that!' she insisted. 'I'm not a marriage wrecker—!'

'Nicole. You are sexy and you are alone. Men will find you irresistible.'

She gave an exasperated sigh. He was exaggerating. But there was some truth in what he said. 'I'll have to shave my hair and wear old clothes,' she said dejectedly.

'That,' Blake commented, 'would be a waste.'

'Perhaps,' she mused, 'my situation brings out men's chivalrous instincts. They want to console me.'

'Perhaps,' he clipped. 'You've certainly suffered over the past months.'

'And worrying about my father's reputation is adding to my worries,' she pointed out softly.

In the silence that followed she knew that Blake was making up his mind about her. So she kept quiet while he did so, hoping he believed that she was absolutely straight in everything she did and that she wasn't defending a monster of a father.

'I think,' he said eventually, 'you might be genuine—'

'Not,' she said, so delighted that she was unable to resist the mischievous impulse, 'a prostitute or a drug user or—'

'Nicole.' He frowned. 'I know I must sound stuffy and cautious, but all my life I've been brought up to protect Cranford and the Bellamie family and to think of its best interests.' His frown deepened. 'Anyone who inherits this land must be prepared to put Cranford before their own needs. That's how it's survived for the past five centuries in the same hands. We have traditions to uphold. Like becoming fluent in French, for instance, merely because our ancestors came from across the Channel.'

'I understand,' she said, contrite. 'You've learnt to weigh your decisions carefully. But you've got things out of all proportion. I'm no threat to Cranford!'

He inhaled deeply as if she might be.

'OK. So you think I was over-reacting. That's because you don't know the problems involved—'

'Then tell me,' she prompted.

'I can't. One day, maybe. But for now, perhaps we both need to know the evidence stacked against your father. If you do stay for a while—'

'Yes?' she asked, her eyes filled with hope.

He eyed her speculatively. 'I'm taking a gamble here. But there's something I must ask of you in return. It entails being…economical with the truth.'

That was unexpected. 'You want me to lie?'

'Not exactly. Let me explain. It seems that fate has thrown us together. And fate has decreed that we might be living in the same house for a time, till we're sure that Luc can travel safely.'

'And you'll get to know me,' she cried eagerly. 'You'll find out that I am an open book—'

'Part of which,' he warned, 'must remain closed.'

She frowned. 'How do you mean?'

'Nicole, I can't let you stay anywhere near this house unless you agree to keep it a secret that we are second cousins. Otherwise I must insist that you and Luc are transferred to a private nursing home some distance away, till you are happy that he's fit for the journey home.'

She didn't want that! She wanted to be with Blake, to learn more about him, to curl up in his arms...

His eyebrow crooked, asking for her agreement, and she forgot her dreams and pulled herself together.

'I'm not sure,' she said slowly. 'I'd be accepting the fact that you're ashamed of me—'

'It's not quite that, Nicole.'

'Then what is it?' she demanded impatiently.

'It's complicated. You realise that I have a sick mother.'

Immediately her expression became sympathetic. 'I do. Josef told me. It must be a terrible worry for you to see her so ill. I remember the feeling exactly.'

'I've had to come to terms with it. There's nothing I can do. To be blunt,' he said, in a horribly tight voice, 'she's dying.'

'How awful!' And now it was her turn to be the consoler. Her turn to stroke his strong, powerful hands. 'Are you very close?' she asked.

His eyes brooded on this. 'She gave up a great deal for me,' he replied quietly.

'That's quite a burden of guilt for you to carry,' Nicole said, unable to hide her disapproval. 'Sacrifice should be willing—and never referred to.'

'You're right, and it *was* like that. In fact, I only learnt about it a short time ago—and she only told me because it was necessary. She loves me very much, Nicole. And I love her.'

'What an awful time for you. I do know how you feel. It's terrible, losing a parent!' she declared passionately.

'Yes. And you'll understand why I didn't want you around, why your arrival shook me. She's very frail and I want her last days to be as peaceful and happy as possible—'

'Of course, but how could I—?'

'Because you're Giles's daughter. And she'd go berserk if she knew you were in the house.'

'She was your source, wasn't she?' Nicole blurted out unhappily. 'She's the one who told you all those lies—'

'She was very certain of what she was saying,' he defended. 'She became almost hysterical when she told me about him. I knew nothing about him until that moment. No one had ever spoken his name or referred to him. There are no photographs or portraits of him. Don't you think that suggests something disastrous must have happened? We Bellamies stick together. And yet this one has been wiped from the family tree—literally.'

She felt helpless. Blake loved his mother. Under the circumstances he'd naturally believe her. Nicole thought that *she'd* even believe the stories if she hadn't known her father so well.

'I don't want to upset you,' she said firmly, 'but she's *wrong*, Blake! Terribly wrong!'

He pulled in a long breath. 'We're going round in circles. I'll suspend judgement till I know for sure, one way or the other. So let's forget for a moment whether she's misguided or not. The point is that she mustn't know anything other than the fact that you are a friend of mine. Anything more will not only hasten her death but she'll die an angry woman.' His voice changed. Became harder, more determined. 'I won't have that. Do you understand?'

She admired his defence of his mother—even though he was wrong. It showed great loyalty.

'I do! Of course you want to protect your mother at this time. And under the circumstances I wouldn't want her upset either!' she cried vehemently.

'So you agree?'

'Absolutely,' she said. 'I'm happy for it to be known

hat I'm a friend, staying for a while. No one else knows of the family connection.'

She would do anything for the sake of the future she wanted to create with him. An excitement skittered within her. She knew she'd disprove those awful stories about her father. And then she and Blake would be free to give rein to their true feelings. Her face became wreathed in smiles.

'Trust me,' she continued, gazing into the dark depths of his eyes. 'For your mother's sake I can keep my mouth shut about our kinship until you want to reveal it.'

He kissed her fingertips, the thickness of his lashes on his cheeks making her heart flutter. 'Thank you!' he murmured with heartfelt relief. Looking up, he gave her a crooked smile. 'Hell. I just hope I'm doing the wise thing—'

'Oh, you are!' she cried happily. 'We'll solve the mystery and we'll become proper cousins. Josef and Luc can get to know one another. Perhaps you can visit us in France in the summer holidays. It'll be lovely, Blake, knowing I have roots, knowing I have family. I can't have wished for anything better.'

It was as if, she thought, delirious with delight, she'd removed an intolerable burden from his shoulders. Leaning forward, he gently kissed her on the mouth.

'You can have the benefit of the doubt—for the time being—kissing cousin.'

'You won't regret this,' she promised him, her eyes starry.

'I hope not. And now—' he declared, leaping energetically to his feet '—I have things to do. Like have a shower and a shave, for a start!' He grinned, suddenly looking carefree. 'Make yourself entirely at home. Mrs Carter starts work at eleven—though Maisie will be around, doing the housework, in case you need anything. You know where

the kitchen is. Make a list of shopping you'll need and it'll
be done for you. Lunch will be at one. I'll see you then—
but tell someone if you're worried about Luc and they'll
reach me on my mobile. OK?'

Nicole nodded, her smile soft and unknowingly inviting
He hesitated, then bent his head and kissed her long
and hard.

'Farewell for now,' he muttered, his breath hot and
harsh against the plushness of her lips.

And then he was off, striding rapidly towards the house.

CHAPTER NINE

THE morning was very relaxing. Free from her fears that Luc was seriously ill and that Blake might throw her out before she had finished her quest, she was able to enjoy herself.

He was going to investigate the rumours about her father. That was progress. So, she thought, brimming with anticipation, was his acknowledgement of the extraordinary chemistry between them. Her fingers tentatively touched her mouth and she sighed, luxuriating in the memory of his kiss. Life suddenly seemed rosy. Blissful, even. She sighed with utter contentment.

Happily she played with Luc, fed and changed him, made herself a hot drink and filched a couple of biscuits from a large cookie jar, then chatted amiably to Mrs Carter. Who had nothing but praise for Blake.

Nicole listened avidly, hugging herself in well-hidden delight as she listened to the tales of Blake's saintliness from infancy to the present day. And, reading between the lines, Nicole picked up a few clues about Blake's wife. Tania had indeed been very beautiful and dreadfully spoilt. And, as Blake had said, it was clear that she'd not been popular in the village.

'Now...' Mrs Carter bustled around, flipping beautifully rolled pastry over a dish of home-bottled peaches and crimping the sides with a surprising deftness. 'That little baby is a lot better. You can hardly see his rash now, so why don't you go for a nice walk while he sleeps here? It's sunny outside and he can stay in the shade of the wisteria outside the kitchen door where I can keep an eye on him. You look as if you need a break and the sun'll do you the world of good.'

'I'd like to,' she demurred, 'but—'

'Go on.' Two hefty hands pushed her towards the open French doors. 'You've got an hour. Then come back for lunch. No argument. You've been devoting all your time to him and no one could fault you as a mother,' she said approvingly. 'But you've got needs too. You'll feel all the better for a good wander in the garden. Mr Blake always does, I know. Likes a bit of freedom, that one.'

'Does he?' She was avid for stories about him. And knew what that hunger implied.

'Always has. He'd get that het up being cooped up indoors when it rained that he'd sneak out and come back hours later, soaked to the skin and muddy but bursting with happiness. He can't be contained for long. Like quicksilver, I always thought. Never happier than when riding or working outside and pretending he's as free as a bird, even though he's got the weight of this place on his shoulders.'

'Was he...?' She hesitated. It seemed as if she was prying. But the cook smiled at her in genial encouragement and so Nicole ventured, 'Was he like his father, or...his second cousin?'

Mrs Carter gave a snort. 'Never like his father! Not for me to speak ill of the dead, but Mr Darcy ran Cranford into the ground. Mr Giles, mind, he was a kindly lad. Polite to me—and I was just a lowly maid in those days.'

'But he left,' Nicole said cautiously, pleased to hear someone speak well of her father at last.

'Some trouble.' Mrs Carter's mouth suddenly buttoned up tight. 'I'll say no more. Family business, not mine. Go on. Have that walk then you'll be up to doing justice to my lunch.'

Nicole laughed, knowing she'd get no further. Another time, she thought. 'You're an angel!' she declared, turning and kissing the plump red cheek. 'Thank you. I'll be back to help with lunch—'

'Don't you trespass on my patch!' cried the cook in horror. 'I'll be out of a job. Get outside. Be off with you. You're under my feet,' she grumbled unconvincingly.

Giggling, Nicole dashed out in mock alarm, turning to wave at the beaming Mrs Carter. How she loved it here! Happily, she wandered through the gardens, admiring the plantings and itching to sketch and paint the views as soon as she had a free minute.

Passing through a wrought iron gate in a high and ancient brick wall, she found herself in a stable yard. In a field beyond she could see several horses grazing, but the sound of irritable snorting and whinnying close by suggested that one stable was still inhabited.

'Hi!' she called to the slim, energetic figure she recognised as Susie.

'Hello!' Susie rushed over, looking anxious. 'How's that baby of yours?'

'Much better, thanks. I think he'll be OK,' Nicole said, touched by Susie's genuine interest. *'Mon Dieu!'* she exclaimed, jumping with fright at the sound of hooves battering the nearest stable door.

'That's Midnight,' Susie explained with a laugh. 'Blake's stallion, complaining because he hasn't been taken out since he was ridden at dawn. He's a devil. No one can manage him except Blake and I leave it to him to put him in the field because Midnight's such a handful. Blake's a whiz with horses. Can do anything with them. They all but lie down and let him tickle their tummies, like dogs! Ah. He's coming.'

Nicole cocked her head to one side but failed to hear anything. 'I'm impressed. You must have ears like a bat!'

'No! The horses have! Look!'

In the field every horse had raised its head and even at

a distance she could see that their ears were pricked forward. Nicole was conscious of the hot breath of Blake's stallion and the restless tossing of its head behind her as it waited impatiently for its master.

Then she saw him riding into view. She held her breath as he approached the gate into the field but his mount cleared it effortlessly. The grazing horses flung up their heads and whinnied in greeting, galloping over to him.

'I wish I had that power,' Susie said enviously. 'He has an affinity with all animals. Wounded birds, injured foxes and badgers, that sort of thing. He's nursed no end of road casualties back to health. Josef has the gift, too. He has no fear and I think animals sense his love for them.'

'In France—' Nicole mused, fascinated by Blake's communication with the horses, which were jostling for his attention '—we'd say someone like that had gypsy blood.'

Susie grinned. 'Well, maybe there's a bit of gypsy blood somewhere. It'd explain his colouring, wouldn't it?'

Nicole giggled. 'The Bellamies would be appalled to hear you say that!'

After a while Blake trotted away, leaning down to open the gate into the yard and jumping down lithely when he arrived, with a look of delight on his face when he saw Nicole was there.

'Hi!' he said cheerfully, busy with unsaddling his mount. Midnight kicked the stable door meaningfully and Blake laughed, his white teeth gleaming in his dark face.

Yes, Nicole thought, seeing something different in those black sparkling eyes and the furiously tousled curls. He does look as if he has a Romany ancestor. Though that couldn't be right because he'd inherited Cranford. There must have been a Mediterranean wife in the Bellamie family long ago, she decided. And reflected that it was interesting how a strong gene could emerge—even, perhaps, after centuries of dormancy.

That might be why she found Blake so intriguing. He was a combination of contrasts... She jumped again as the stable door received a flurry of angry kicks.

'I'll deal with Flouncy,' Susie said to Blake, taking the reins. 'You sort that one out.'

He laughed again. 'Midnight or Nicole?'

Susie giggled. 'Take your pick!'

'Flouncy?' queried Nicole with mock horror, in retaliation.

'Josef's choice.'

She grinned. 'Might have guessed!' But it described the horse very well. It did flounce.

'It's good to see you here,' Blake murmured, ignoring the snorting beast trying to batter down the reinforced stable door.

Nicole felt her heart beat faster. He looked so alive. Sweat beaded his forehead. His eyes gleamed, his face glowed with vibrant health. And there was something so achingly sexy about his crisp white shirt, tight jodhpurs and high boots that her throat closed up in sheer longing.

'I imagine Luc's better or you wouldn't be here,' he said when she didn't speak.

'Much improved,' she said huskily. 'The rash has nearly vanished.'

For a moment her radiant face stopped him in his tracks. 'I'm very, very pleased,' he said, smiling idiotically at her.

Susie threw him a towel and he busied himself with wiping his sweaty face and hands. It gave him something to do. He would have preferred to grab Nicole and kiss her and think of doing unspeakable things to her. Instead of quietening his passions, the ride had made them fiercer. He wanted her with an all-consuming urgency. Dangerous ground, his common sense told him prissily. Why not? every other sense replied.

Earlier on he'd issued that ultimatum to her—that she

wasn't to set foot on his land—because he'd been appalled by his lust for a woman who might be something of a harlot.

But his feelings about her had changed. He did believe her to be essentially kind and innocent of the effect she had on men. That old friend of his, common sense, had told him to steer clear, to let well alone. But his gut feelings had rebelled. And morally he knew he couldn't just send her home. He must learn more about her. And her father.

It had disturbed him how happy that decision had made him. It was as if he had opened a door and let the light shine in. This time he *was* doing the right thing. His troubled conscience would rest in peace.

However, he had no intention of telling her that he was a bastard—yet. If she proved to be the daughter of a rogue, if she had inherited some of Giles's unpleasant traits, then he could send her packing without endangering the estate and its dependants.

However, if she was above suspicion... He put the towel down on the mounting block with a slow deliberation. Then he didn't know what he'd do. How could he leave? Josef would be desolate...

'Blake!' yelled Susie. 'Stop staring at that yukky towel and see to that brute of yours!'

'Sorry. Miles away.' He glanced up at Nicole, who seemed to be looking at him with some curiosity. 'Won't be a minute,' he said with unreal jollity. Quite fearless of the flying hooves of his ill-tempered stallion, he unbolted the stable door.

'I don't know much about horses,' Nicole called nervously, backing away.

'Wise to stand clear of this one,' he cried in warning over his shoulder.

As usual, Midnight skittered out in a blur of gleaming

black muscle and flailing hooves while Blake tried to keep his grip on the bridle and his feet on the ground. As usual, Blake felt awed by the animal's beauty and thrilled and privileged that the spirited horse regarded him as a friend to be trusted.

'Gently, gently,' he soothed, stroking with a mesmeric rhythm. There was a token toss of a powerful head, a low hrrumph, and then Midnight was all his. 'I know,' he whispered, snuffling into his stallion's nostrils. 'You hate being cooped up. Me, too. But you needed a long rest after our ride last night. Come on.'

At a run, he led the now reasonably docile Midnight to the field and set him free. With the gate safely closed, Nicole came to join him.

'He's fabulous,' she marvelled as Midnight kicked and bucked his way around the field in sheer joy of living.

'Pure Arab. My indulgence,' he replied, following the glorious shift of muscle beneath the racehorse flanks. There was something uplifting about Midnight's exhilaration. It touched a chord in him. He, too, could set himself free. He could run wild if he wanted. He could rip off the imposed restrictions that he had railed against for years and follow his impulses, like Nicole.

He shot her a sideways glance. The wind was blowing silken strands of hair over her face. Eyes fixed on the now cantering Midnight, she lifted a graceful hand and her long tapering fingers absently tucked the hair behind her small ear.

Her face was uplifted, the sun lighting her high cheekbones and the inviting curves of her breasts. An ache hit him so hard that he had to grit his teeth and turn away. He was hot and sweaty. This wasn't the time.

Angrily he glared at Midnight, envying him the freedom he denied himself. He took a deep breath. To hell with denial! He knew what he wanted. And he wanted it *now*!

'Come.'

Without waiting for her agreement, he caught her hand and led her through the yard and up the steps of the hayloft.

'What…?' She took one look at the piles of sweet-smelling hay and the penny dropped. 'Why, Mr Blake!' she murmured with a good mimicry of a country wench. 'What can be in your mind, sir?'

'You,' he growled with a curt impatience.

Her eyes grew huge and melting. The smile that parted her lips was mischievous and utterly ravishing.

'I'm so glad,' she said huskily, and held out her arms.

Roughly, he pulled her to him. Bent her supple spine with the ferocity of his kiss. Pushed her back to the straw where they fell. Felt blood surge through his body when he lay on her, kissing her with a sweet passion that made him want to groan.

And she urged him on with wicked words in his ear, telling him what she liked, what she wanted, refusing to allow him to hold back because she needed his passion to match hers.

His head was whirling. He couldn't think, couldn't order his body to obey him any more. This was truly making love. No studied moves. Just pure and perfect harmony of one body with another, with hands, lips, teeth, exacting the greatest pleasure.

The softness of her skin awed him. When his lips brushed her midriff it was like feeling the smoothness of satin. Somehow she was naked—though he couldn't say how—and his shirt had been dispensed with, so that they were skin to skin and he could feel the hectic thunder of his own heart and the rapid pounding of hers.

She tasted so sweet. He couldn't get enough of her

mouth, even as her legs twisted around his and the heat of her made him cry out in need. Her fingers deftly hooked open his jodhpurs and he felt her hands caressing the tight, hard muscles of his buttocks.

She was beautiful. Unbelievably, heart-stoppingly desirable.

'Nicole,' he said thickly, dazed, bewildered by the frightening power of his rioting emotions.

There was a little flicker of her tongue and she licked the corner of his mouth. A huge shudder went through him and then another as she slid her hand down and touched him. He couldn't wait. He had to tell her so...

'I—can't—I—'

His eyes closed. He was there. Warm, liquid, welcome. And then he took his freedom, suddenly elated, intoxicated with it, sharing himself with Nicole, knowing only the gloriously liberating movement of their bodies as they united and the unstoppable joy that flooded every cell, every inch of his being.

Nicole jerked as a series of unbearably exquisite spasms rewarded her body. Blake looked down at her, unshed tears making his eyes glisten. And at that moment she fell head over heels in love with him. She read his heart in those longing, loving eyes. And knew that she would be bound to him for the rest of her life. Whatever happened.

'Oh, my darling!' he whispered, touching her face tenderly, wonderingly. 'I'm sorry. I was too—'

Her finger pressed against his lips. Panting with exertion, weak with love and satiation, she smiled her radiant smile. 'It was perfect. Hot, hard, furious. So much passion. Wonderful,' she breathed.

Gently he bent his head, his hair tumbling over his forehead in glistening black curls and she was reminded of the stallion—impatient, angry and frustrated then full of joy to be free. They were both dark, both touched with the same magic and powerful masculinity. Creatures who needed space and no restrictions if they were to flourish.

Blake's mouth claimed hers in a long and tender kiss. Her arms wrapped around his neck and she sighed into it. His liquid black eyes danced with happiness and she felt thrilled to be the cause of it. With the lightest of touches he caressed her face and throat, his finger drawing a path between her breasts. As his tongue lapped the beads of milk quivering on the peak of each nipple, she caught hold of his thick, tousled hair and moaned with pleasure, saying in a reluctant whisper, 'I should go. Feed Luc. It must be late—'

Blake groaned. 'Time! It's the enemy of lovers. I want to stay here all afternoon with you. But…yes. I must shower and spend some time with my mother before lunch. I promised.'

'Yes,' she said, but he kissed her and wouldn't let her go. 'Blake.' Gently she pushed him away. 'I must go!' she said with reluctance.

'You know what you've done,' he said huskily.

Her heart seemed to bounce. 'Yes!' she whispered.

He smiled and hauled up his jodhpurs. 'I wonder if you do. The way I feel at the moment, I'm going to want to be with you twenty-four hours a day and I'll resent any time spent elsewhere.'

She giggled with delight and hurriedly dressed, stopping every few seconds to fend off his kisses. 'You're insatiable!' she pretended to protest as his mouth enclosed hers once more.

'Driven crazy by a witch of a woman,' he growled and stood still in evident bliss as her hands slowly shaped the beautiful contours of his chest.

'Blake,' she whispered, hugging him tight, 'I'm so glad we found one another.'

With lowered lashes, he smoothed back her hair, for all

the world as if he were a fussy hairdresser with a client. 'There. You'll do.' A kiss was dropped on her lips and then he was drawing her to the barn door.

As she hurried back to the house alone it seemed that her heart was full to bursting. So she sang and let her happiness ring out across the garden. Not long ago she'd been in despair. Now... She had never felt so content in the whole of her life.

CHAPTER TEN

BLAKE felt guilty at his sense of relief when he finally left his mother. But she'd questioned him about Nicole with surprising vigour for someone so ill. And he'd hated not being honest with her. It seemed a betrayal, somehow.

God, he was torn! Josef had always come first in everything. Before his duty, before his mother, before Cranford itself. And now, in even contemplating the idea that Nicole might one day guide little Luc to his rightful inheritance, he could be throwing away his son's future. Let alone his own.

In turmoil, raging against his mother's lover despite the fact that the man had given him life, he strode with a grim, rapid gobbling of the ground towards the idyllic scene beneath the cedar tree.

A light lunch had been set there. Nicole sprawled on a rug beside the old teak table with its snowy white cloth and assorted cold dishes. As he approached, his stride and his temper mellowed. Magic.

The fact that she turned to smile at him just melted away his hammering problems. She could do to him, he mused, what he could do to Midnight. Soothe the savage breast. Make everything seem all right.

He'd changed into a short-sleeved summer shirt the colour of pollen and had scrambled into a pair of faded old jeans. Dropping down beside her, he peered at the naked little baby on the changing mat. Luc was crowing happily and waving his arms and legs in glee.

Blake smiled at the perfection of the child and then at Nicole. 'He looks fine. I can't see any rash.'

She tickled Luc's tummy and was rewarded with a chortle. Her beatific smile reached the depths of Blake's heart. 'Isn't it wonderful? I think he'll get the all-clear when the doctor calls,' she said happily.

He let Luc grip his finger, enchanted by the gurgling child. 'Such a tiny body,' he marvelled. 'It's amazing to think he'll grow into an adult. A miracle.'

The heir to Cranford, he thought with a pang. And frowned because he couldn't wish this child anything but a full and happy life. Did that mean granting him his birthright?

'Can I hold him?' he asked, by way of apology to the little boy. 'I remember when Joe was this small. I felt choked up every time I saw him. I couldn't believe he was my son and kept creeping up to touch him to make sure he was real.'

'Be my guest,' she said softly. And she leaned over and kissed his cheek.

He caught her face in his hands, turning it so that he could taste her mouth. She smelt of baby. That fresh, talcum smell. Her hair...he nuzzled her neck...reminded him of apple blossom scent. Her skin...was all woman.

Before things went too far he pulled away. Picked up the squirming little Luc and cuddled the plump bottom in the palm of his hand. Blue eyes stared at him trustingly. He felt a swoop of love which mingled with a very large twist of guilt.

'He's gorgeous,' he said huskily.

'Mm.'

It was a strange sound that had come from Nicole. She'd turned away and seemed to be unnecessarily fiddling with things in the baby bag. Tucking Luc over one shoulder with reckless regard for the consequences, Blake reached out his hand and gently drew her to face him. Her eyes

were glistening and she looked as if she might be struggling for composure.

'There's no need to be sad,' he said, caressing her face.

She pushed her fists, child-like, against her eyes and
found a smile for him. 'I'm not. I just go to pieces when
I see a strong, masculine male with a tiny baby in his arms.
It's so poignant, so sweet.' She laughed. 'I know! I'm an
idiot! But it's lovely to see you adoring Luc. Shall we have
lunch?' she added lightly, jumping up.

It wasn't possible for her to tell him that she'd felt a
visceral tug of motherhood. That she wanted to have
Blake's babies. Wanted him to cherish and love her and
their children. What on earth, she wondered, appalled with
herself for such fantasies, would he say to all that? Probably run a mile and ban her from England itself, let alone
Cranford!

'Now. How was your mother?' she asked briskly when
Luc had been deposited on the mat again and Blake had
come to sit at the table beside her.

'Suspicious,' he replied drily.

Nicole's eyes widened. 'Why?' she asked, cutting herself a slice of quiche.

He grinned ruefully. 'Even after I'd showered and
changed I think I must still have been glowing rather more
than usual. To be honest, I felt as if I could conquer the
world and still dance the night away, I felt so good. I
suppose it showed. She all but put me under a searchlight
to interrogate me!'

Nicole's eyes sparkled with amusement and delight.
'What did you say?'

Blake concentrated on transferring a fillet of cold
salmon on to his plate. 'I told her a bit about you. I think
she put two and two together. My offhand, casual tone
didn't fool her a bit. She knows me well. She knew I was

still flying. And guessed we'd become lovers.' He shot a
questioning glance at her. 'Do you mind?'

'I don't, no. We're free agents, we can do what we like.
But does *she* mind?' She was pleased when he leaned forward and kissed her. His hand stroked her arm. She heaved
a happy sigh.

'I don't think so. She's probably glad to see me happy.'
His hand dropped away. 'That's all we want for our children, isn't it?' he added, suddenly frowning at a baby tomato on his plate as if it had no right to be there.

She had to touch him, to reassure this mercurial, com-
plex man. Her fingers slid over his shoulder, felt the taut-
ness of the muscle running to his neck then teased the
small tendrils of defiant hair which curled so appealingly
at the nape despite all his attempts to control them.

With encouragement from her he had released his emotions. Had flung himself into a kind of abyss that was
unknown. Although he'd surrendered joyfully and whole-
heartedly to his instincts he would naturally find it unnerving to abandon all those years of self-restraint.

'We owe it to our children to be happy, too,' she murmured in his ear.

'Sometimes—' he said in a low tone, disappointing her
by not responding more enthusiastically '—that may not
be possible.'

'Are you talking of your mother's sacrifice for you? Has
she led an unhappy life?' she asked gently. 'I can't believe
that to be true. She loves you and has seen you grow into
a man she must be proud of. And there's Josef, too, surely
the apple of her eye—'

'Yes. Of course,' he said roughly, but there was pain in
his voice.

From his grim profile she knew he was keeping something from her. Something important—perhaps connected
with his mother's illness. That meant he didn't trust her.

Unaccountably distressed by this, she reached over and kissed him lightly on the corner of his tense mouth.

'Your mother's not the only one who doesn't like to see you unhappy,' she said quietly.

He shot her a quick look and suddenly his mouth was full on hers, searching, demanding and desperate. 'Nicole,' he whispered throatily. 'Nicole!'

Loving him, she responded passionately, hoping that he'd forget his worries for a short while and find solace in her.

'Better?' she murmured when they broke apart for a moment.

'Sure.' He flashed her a smile that wasn't entirely believable. 'Let's eat. We've a lot to do this afternoon.'

'Have we?' she asked brightly.

There wasn't any point in pushing Blake to confide in her. She could wait. But the disappointment sat sourly in her stomach.

'If you'd like to.'

He was getting further and further from her every second. She bit her lip. 'Doing what?'

His fork idly toyed with the salmon. 'I thought you might like to come with me on my rounds. Things I need to do on the estate,' he said casually.

She beamed. That was inclusive enough. 'I'd enjoy that. I'll need to sort Luc out first and settle him for his sleep—'

'We'll leave him with Mrs Carter,' Blake said firmly. 'There'll be a lot of getting in and out of the car and chatting to people. OK?'

'Providing she doesn't mind—' she began, looking doubtful.

He looked directly at her. 'I want you to come. It's important to me.'

'Oh!' She felt flustered by this admission. 'Then…yes. Of course. I'm sure Luc will be in good hands.'

When they'd finished eating she dressed Luc and curled up on the rug with him on her lap. Quite unselfconsciously she began to feed him while Blake waited.

'All done, sweetheart?' she murmured to her sleepy baby and gently tucked him in his buggy. 'Right,' she said, straightening and slowly buttoning herself up. 'Oh!'

Blake followed her surprised gaze and stared at the house, his eyes narrowed. 'What is it?' he asked warily.

'A face. At an upstairs window.' She blushed, hating to be spied on.

'What kind of a face—and where?' he retorted.

'I just saw white hair. See where the coat of arms is? Well above that and two windows to the left.'

Blake frowned. 'My mother.'

She heaved a sigh of relief. 'That's all right, then! She must be feeling better.'

'Or insatiably curious,' he drawled.

'I should think she reckons I'm rather shocking, feeding Luc in front of you,' Nicole mused. And she looked at him in sudden alarm. 'I did want to make a good impression,' she complained. 'And now if she ever finds out who I am, she'll think—'

'She won't find out who you are!' Blake hurled with a sudden sharpness. 'She mustn't.' There was a cold silence and then he said a little more calmly, 'Now, if you're ready, we'll make a start.'

She hung her head. He was so distant and stern suddenly. Her day was blighted. But she had to hold on, to give him space. She loved him enough to do that.

He felt as if he was walking a tightrope. One that stretched far into the distance with no end in sight. And he swayed from one side to another—surrendering to his wild passions one moment and jerking himself back into his old, suppressed self the next.

But the next few hours would extend his knowledge of Nicole. His tenants were direct and called a spade a spade. Maybe he was blinded by sexual longing, but they'd suss her out.

Back at the house, he packed a box of peaches into the four-wheel drive together with a pile of magazines and several romances he'd bought from a village stall the previous week, then flung in his overalls. Nicole chattered cheerfully as they drove to their first call—Mrs Lee in the small ex-gamekeeper's cottage. He answered tersely, increasingly nervous about the outcome.

He realised that he wanted her to be accepted by everyone. That was madness, of course. If she was as pure as the driven snow then he'd have no choice but to vacate the seat of lord of the manor. It would suit his purpose, he scowled, if she made a complete hash of this afternoon and then he could pack her off home none the wiser.

Except that if she went he'd feel as if his right arm had been torn off and minced for cat food.

Hell. He ground the gears and irritably fought with them. For the first time in his life, after being renowned for crisp, wise decisions, he couldn't even make up his darn mind.

'Mrs Lee,' he said crisply to the strangely silent Nicole as they bounced down the narrow track and the cottage came in sight. He ignored her huge, soulful eyes and concentrated on the job in hand. 'Courtesy visit. She's elderly and doesn't get out much.'

'Oh. Are the novels and magazines for her? Shall I bring them—?'

'No. She'd think I was playing Lord Bountiful.' He drew to a halt. 'Leave them where they are.'

After handing Nicole out he wiped the frown from his face and walked with her to the door, pulling the old-fashioned bell pull as he'd done so many times throughout his life. There was the sound of shuffling and a quavering voice called out, 'Who is it?'

'The wicked wolf, Goldilocks!' Blake shouted cheerily.

'Rascal!' Chuckling, Mrs Lee opened the door and lifted her gaunt cheek for his kiss.

'Hope you don't mind. I was on my way to the village with my friend—Nicole—and I thought I'd just drop by to see if you needed anything while I'm shopping there.'

'I might,' she replied with dignity. 'There again, I might not. How do you do, Nicole? Come in. I'll make us some tea.'

He saw Nicole's warm, ready smile emerge and charm the old lady. 'Thank you. I'd love some,' she enthused.

Full marks, Blake approved. She didn't offer to make the tea for Mrs Lee. The old lady was fiercely independent and Nicole hadn't made that mistake.

'Don't know of anyone who'd take some books and things off my hands, do you?' he enquired, when they were all nursing steaming mugs of tea strong enough for a mouse to trot on. 'My mother's read them and I'm supposed to take them to a boot fair but I haven't the time.'

'Might. Let's have a look,' Mrs Lee said cautiously.

He hid a smile and dutifully hurried out, taking his time to stack the books in a neat pile on top of the magazines. When he returned Mrs Lee was squealing with laughter at something Nicole had said. He waited in the hall, fascinated.

'I'm a bit paranoid about it now.' She was giggling as the old lady rasped her delight. 'I don't think I'll ever wear a baby sling again, for fear of being taken for Quasimodo's sister!'

Of course. The episode with Josef. He grinned, remembering it. And his first glimpse of Nicole, the first time he'd ever been socked between the eyes by a woman, never to recover.

'Smashing kiddie,' declared Mrs Lee. 'Like his Dad. Never liked the father, though. The cousin, though, that was a different kettle of fish.'

Blake froze. She was talking about Giles.

'You remember them both, do you, Mrs Lee?' Nicole asked and he could hear the tension in her voice even though she'd tried to sound casual.

'Mr Darcy was an arrogant little pup,' grumbled Mrs Lee. 'Glad to see the back of him. Mr Giles was kinder, a real gentleman. Liked to paint, I remember. Did that portrait for me, up there. It's unfinished; that's why it's unsigned. But it's his all right.'

He heard the swish of Nicole's skirt and reckoned she'd gone to look. He knew the painting well but he had had no idea who had painted it. It was of Mrs Lee as a younger woman. He'd always admired it. There'd been a running joke where he'd make some ridiculous offer for it—five hundred thousand pounds, usually—and she'd regally refuse, saying she liked it and what would she do with all that money, anyway?

'It's…'

Blake swallowed. Nicole's voice had cracked. She would have recognised her father's work. And she'd feel upset. It was a beautiful portrait of Mrs Lee, depicting her as a handsome and generous-natured woman, done with love and feeling. The work, he'd always felt, of a man with perception and insight, who had seen beneath the skin and bone and somehow teased out the real nature of the person during the sitting.

'It's excellent,' Nicole said tenderly. 'He's captured the real you.'

'You can see it, can't you? I know a kindred spirit when I see one. That's why Mr Giles and I got on. We were all very fond of him. Pity he had to go abroad so suddenly.

Never came back. Never finished my painting.' She cackled. 'He wouldn't recognise me now, would he?'

'Actually, I think he would,' Nicole said quietly. 'You're the same inside, aren't you? And that's what he saw.'

'Clever girl.' There was the sound of a hand being patted. 'Now. Where's that young man of yours? He hasn't finished his tea.'

'He's not my—' Nicole began as Blake tiptoed back to the front door, intending to make a noise coming in.

'You can't fool me. I saw how he looked at you. I hope he snaps you up before someone else does— Ah. Here he is.'

'Sorry to be so long,' Blake announced, his mind teeming with strands of thought. 'Had to sort out the sexy ones—'

'Oh, I like those!' protested the old lady.

He gave her a withering look. 'I know. Those are the ones I sorted out for you! I left behind the books with a sweet aproned figure on the front. You've got any which show passionate clinches and rippling muscles.'

The two women laughed and exchanged girly glances. Blake had to award Nicole maximum points on the visit. Mrs Lee was notoriously blunt and could tell false smarm from forty paces.

As he joked and defended himself against the combined forces of the women he reflected that his eavesdropping had been an eye-opener. Perhaps his mother *was* mistaken. He felt a ridiculous surge of happiness at the thought and wondered why on earth he was merrily advancing towards his own ejection from Cranford. Then he looked at the laughing Nicole and knew.

And the revelation came as a terrible shock.

CHAPTER ELEVEN

'IT's compelling evidence,' he agreed when Nicole excitedly told him of the conversation with Mrs Lee while he was supposedly out in the car sorting the books. 'I'll talk to my mother. Try to get to the bottom of this.'

'Oh,' she cried, clasping her hands together in delight. 'Thank you, Blake! Thank you!'

'Blacksmith next,' he announced, controlling the urge to first stop the car and kiss her parted lips and then rush back to confront his mother. 'He's teaching me his craft.'

'Why?' she asked in surprise.

Because he loved it. Felt a stirring in his soul when he hammered out the softened, malleable iron. When sheer physical labour and an unerring eye resulted in a work of lasting beauty and usefulness.

'Why not? I'll be about an hour. That's all he'll allow me of his time,' he said with a grin. 'The potter's nearby, or you can wander around the village if you're bored—'

'I'll watch you for a while, see what a mess you make of things,' she teased. 'Then I'll do those bits of shopping for Mrs Lee.'

Nicole shook hands with the short, stocky Joseph Croxford, the blacksmith, who looked just a little older than Blake. Her hand was dwarfed by the man's huge fist but his handshake was gentle and his smile welcoming.

While Blake stripped off his clothes somewhere in the backyard and shrugged on his overalls and a heavy leather apron like Joseph's she looked around with interest. It was dark inside the small, high-roofed barn and, peering in the gloom, she could see tools of all kinds hanging from the timber and plaster walls.

'How long has the forge been here?' she asked Joseph.

'Long time.' He picked up a heavy hammer. 'Been Croxford blacksmiths and master blacksmiths in the village for hundreds of years,' he said proudly as Blake came in the back door. 'Long before those upstart Bellamies wandered in, anyhow.'

She laughed as Blake threw Joseph a mock glare. 'Newcomers, are they?' she sympathised.

'Furriners. Came over from Calais. We're mentioned in the Doomsday Book,' the blacksmith replied.

'As sheep stealers, if I remember,' grinned Blake.

'Prob'ly right.' Joseph chuckled. 'Least my family has decent English names, not fancy furrin ones. Your mother had sense, not calling you Darcy.'

'Or Giles,' Nicole offered.

'Don't know that one. Here. Grab that rod, Mr Blake, and see if you can make more'n a pig's ear out of it.'

For all their joshing the men were comfortable with one another, Nicole realised. She leaned against the grimy wall and watched them. Blake had pulled his overalls up to his waist and tied the sleeves in a knot there, leaving his chest bare. Soon it was glistening with sweat as he worked at the white-hot forge.

Scarlet sparks flew into the air and the sound of a bell-like ringing resounded around the small forge as he beat the rod into shape on the massive anvil. There was something wonderfully primitive about the scene.

Blake could have been any ordinary man from any time down the centuries, skilfully fashioning everyday items from a lump of metal. She watched him, crazy with love for him, tenderly smiling at his deeply engrossed expression as he struggled to meet Joseph's exacting standards.

'Relax your grip, man!' bellowed the smith. 'Let the

hammer bounce! And stop checking with your audience for approval,' he grumbled.

Blake seemed to redden, though it could have been the light from the fire.

'How's he doing?' she whispered when the smith collected a huge pair of pliers from the bench nearby.

'Not bad for an amateur.' Joseph paused. 'Heard about your father. Must have been hard for you. He can't have been very old,' he said with surprising gentleness.

Nicole looked into the thoughtful grey eyes. 'He wasn't. It was cancer,' she explained quietly.

'Like mine too, lass. Comes hard to see them go like that.' He hesitated. 'Like me to make a cross and put it under the old yew?'

She felt overwhelmed by his kindness. 'I'd like that very much,' she said quietly. 'Tell me what it would cost and—'

'I don't charge Mr Blake's friends. This place would be about my ears if it wasn't for him. You'll do me a favour in return, one day.'

'But… I live in France,' she began uncertainly.

'At the moment,' Joseph said, moving away. And, before she could ask him what he meant, he yelled at Blake, 'Come on you, put your back into it! Can't hang about all day—'

'Tyrant! I'll put your rent up,' Blake yelled back over the din as his hammer flew up and down in a silvery arc.

'Don't pay none!' cried Joseph triumphantly.

Blake paused and flashed a dazzling grin at them both. 'Forgot!' Laughing, he drew his forearm across his brow and left streaks of dirt there. He was panting, his chest heaving, and never had he looked more desirable.

She caught Joseph's sharp, speculative eyes on her and hoped he hadn't identified the naked adoration in her eyes. To show how casual she felt, she reluctantly decided to leave. 'I'm going to the shop!' she shouted at Blake, who'd resumed his hammering.

He thrust the bar into the fiery embers. 'Wander round the village, too. I'll meet you in the pub. Three o'clock.'

'How did you get on?' he asked when she walked into the old pub ten minutes late. Though he knew very well.

She'd been accepted. Taken to the hearts of those villagers she'd met. Joseph, Joan who ran the shop and several locals who'd been shopping there, Tim the potter... His heart thudded at the implications.

She came to sit with him on the high-backed settle and gave her version of events while the darts team roared one another on in the background.

Fresh from his naked dunking under Joseph's cold tap in the back yard and a vigorously applied scrubbing brush, he leaned back with his pint glass of well-earned local apple juice and watched her enthusiastically reporting on the friendliness of everyone in Great Aston.

'Can I get you a drink?' he asked politely when she paused for breath.

'Something soft, please. Same as you?'

She smiled and nodded in a friendly way at a group of farmers at the bar. To a man, they raised their glasses to her and she beamed as if they'd presented her with rubies.

Perhaps they had, he thought, weathering the farmers' comments as he waited to be served. This one afternoon's success could result in her controlling Cranford's fortunes.

'Get your own French lessons,' he retorted drily to a risqué comment about her presence from one of the farmers. He hurried back across the stone-flagged floor to where she sat. 'I've got some fences to check and then I thought we'd go into the hills after,' he said casually.

'Erm...what's happening there?' she asked, checking her watch.

'Sex,' he retorted. 'I'm going to make love to you. I'm managing to keep my hands off you for the moment but soon I'll be forced to touch you. Kiss you all over—'

'Blake,' she said, sounding wonderfully husky, 'I'd like nothing more. But I have to get back soon to feed Luc.'

He screwed his eyes tightly shut. Took a few deep breaths. Swigged his juice. Tried not to let that unpleasant little voice intrude and tell him that she was evading him and keeping him dangling.

'Of course. I'll just take another cold shower. Sit in a freezer for a week or two. Don't mind me.'

She giggled. 'They say anticipation is sweet.'

'They're wrong. It's agony,' he growled, dumping his glass on the table.

Her eyes flirted outrageously. He was conscious that everyone was looking at them and he didn't care. Leaning forwards, he took her face between his hands and gave her a long, slow kiss.

Somewhere in the background the farmers were making encouraging noises. He didn't need their encouragement. He was doing fine all by himself.

'To hell with anticipation,' he muttered.

'Now you've done it!' she breathed. 'The entire village will know what you've been up to.'

He touched her sultry mouth. Lusted after her straining breasts. Knew that he was captivated by her, caught hook, line and sinker. In that moment he decided to throw away the rule book and to 'wing' it. He'd follow his instincts and his impulses and see what happened.

And the moment he could, he'd turn the searchlight on his mother and interrogate *her*. As far as the problem of himself and Josef being turned out on the streets was concerned, he'd solve that somehow. There *must* be an answer. If only his chaotic brain could come up with it...

*   *   *

Thwarted by his mother's worrying relapse after her venture to the window, he had stayed by her bed for a long time after dinner, talking to her about the events of the day.

But he couldn't ask her about Giles. She seemed too frail to be questioned. His mind whirled and whirled until he felt as if he'd been in a tumble-drier for a week and all his brain cells had been spun dry.

'How is she?' Looking anxious, Nicole jumped up from the sofa where she'd been waiting for him.

'Asleep, and much better after I made her laugh by giving her a blow-by-blow account of Josef's beetles,' he said with an absent smile.

Nicole chuckled and sank elegantly back against the pale damask cushions, her long dress a vivid, life-affirming streak of red.

'Dung beetles!' she murmured fondly.

He thought of his beloved son, sleeping innocently upstairs, unaware that his future hung in the balance. He had to turn away because his heart had wrenched so fiercely that he couldn't hide his anguish.

Josef had been home from school when they returned from dropping off the shopping for Mrs Lee. He'd met them with a joyous welcome, squealing that Luc wasn't spotty at all and did that mean he could show him and Nicole his beetles.

'I'm only keeping them for a bit,' he'd explained when Nicole had solemnly agreed. 'Animals need to be free. They like to be outside finding their own dung, you see.'

Of course Blake had already seen Josef enthusiastically demonstrating the technique used by the beetles as they rolled and heaved the dung across fields that must be the size of Britain to them, but he still found the performance very funny. And he'd noticed Nicole wasn't daring to look at him because she must surely have been convulsed with laughter inside.

Ironically, the perfect day had only made things worse. She'd gone down a storm. Josef doted on her. Elderly ladies softened at the sight of her. Old men dreamed of their youth when they looked into her eyes and found themselves eagerly engaged in a conversation about their personal interests.

He doubted that anyone would mind if she replaced him. He went cold. And forced himself to face reality. Pictured Josef's bewildered, tear-stained face as they drove away from Cranford, never to return.

His guts twisted. No. He couldn't do that to his child!

There *was* an answer, of course. He could have his cake and eat it. His conscience would be salved if he said nothing and she stayed as his mistress. Then Josef would inherit and perhaps half the estate could be settled on Luc.

But it was such a momentous decision that he dared not risk making a fool of himself without giving it cold, deliberate thought. She might refuse, of course. The thought gnawed at him, churning away inside and ruining his digestion. Too much rested on this. For Josef's sake, he must not make another mistake in his love life.

'Come and kiss me,' she murmured softly.

His resolve almost melted away. He gritted his teeth. Knowingly or not, she was seducing him, inch by inch, softening his brain and, for his son's sake, he needed a clear head. Brains that worked, not loins.

'No time,' he said shortly. Fiddling busily with his gold cuff-links, he tried not to feel the sudden chill in the atmosphere. 'I'm going over to see the fireworks in a minute. Want to come?' he asked casually.

'What's the matter?' she countered in an anxious voice.

'Nothing.'

'Liar. You're worried about your mother, aren't you?' she said gently.

He groaned. He'd heard the swish of her silky dress as she rose. The soft pad of her feet. The warmth and the scent of her that told him she was near.

She came to lay her head against his chest. He stroked the gleaming cornfield hair, wishing there wasn't this terrible secret between them.

'All you can do—' she said in her soft, soothing voice '—is to make her as comfortable and as happy as possible. Show her you'll be all right when...when she's gone. That's what my father worried about. I told him how I'd manage and put his mind at rest. So make sure she knows you have everything you want.'

'But I don't,' he muttered.

Innocently she gazed up at him. 'What else could you possibly want?'

'You!' he growled and took her mouth by storm. 'Come and dance with me,' he urged thickly. 'I want to hold you in my arms in public. To feel your body against mine, like this... To look into your eyes and know that you need me as much as I need you.'

'The children—' she gasped, as stunned as he was by his outburst.

'Maisie is sleeping next to the nursery tonight and babysitting Josef.' He grinned lopsidedly. 'Or it could be the other way round! I knew I'd be putting in an appearance at the dancing and the firework display. She'll be thrilled to be in charge of Luc, too. He sleeps well. He'll come to no harm.' He brushed his lips against her cheek. Nuzzled the softness of her neck. 'Is it a date?' he asked, barely able to breathe for hoping.

Her mouth found his. And then she was dreamily smiling into his eyes.

'Only if you take your mobile so Maisie can reach you

in any emergency,' she murmured, her fingers wonderingly stroking his face.

Hand in hand they wandered across the gardens to the orangerie. Everyone seemed to be looking at them when they walked into the crowded room. He knew that the men were openly admiring Nicole and he felt a kick of pride that she was with him—and that her sparkling eyes and delighted smile were for him, and him only.

Whatever the future brought, he knew that he wanted Nicole now. He would do what his mother had suggested. Follow his heart.

Concealing his impatience, he introduced Nicole to the organisers and the dignitaries. Then managed to slip away with her, leading her to the dance floor. Taking her in his arms, he felt utterly content with life. As if he'd started to be himself. The soft silk of her dress flowed warmly against him, the heat of her body penetrating the thin material as she responded to the sensual blues rhythm. He had eyes only for her. She for him.

The room didn't exist. Just the two of them. Her heart beating against his chest. The pounding of his heart echoing in his head. Her slender, supple body in the enclosing circle of his arm, bending with his every movement as if they were glued together in an inseparable bond.

Her breathing sounded as short and shallow and as laboured as his. The scent of her was driving him crazy. The slipping of her body, as she swayed languorously to the music, rubbed provocatively against his aching, burning loins. Every time she encountered the hardness of him she gave a little shudder of suppressed delight.

He must ask her. Now.

'Nicole.' Huskily he whispered into her ear. Half-afraid, unsure. They'd only known one another for a short time. He had nothing to lose by asking her to be his mistress. But did she?

'Mmm?'

Her smile dazzled him. She was wonderful, he thought lazily.

'I feel I've known you all my life,' he marvelled, still blinded by her shining eyes and happy smile.

'That's how I feel about you,' she said with a sigh.

'You know I want you!' he said urgently.

A mischievous glance. 'I had noticed!'

'I mean... Nicole, there's something I want to say. Will you come somewhere private with me?' he said huskily.

She nodded, wondering affectionately why he didn't just tell her that he wanted to make love to her. In a blissful daze, she let herself be tucked against his hip and led out of the orangerie. His arm lay heavily around her shoulders and he seemed tense. She'd relax him soon, she thought happily.

They stopped by the lake. It was still and an inky black, except where the moonlight was turning it to silver. The scent of honeysuckle was almost overpowering her senses.

He turned her to him and kissed her, long and hard, and she stood on tiptoe, her hands clasped around his beautiful head to intensify the pressure of their mouths. It seemed they kissed for hours, unable to get enough of one another's mouths.

I love him, she thought, beginning to feel as if she was floating.

'Nicole.' It was barely a whisper in her ear.

'Will you...' He drew in a shuddering breath as she looked deeply into his eyes, telling him yes, she would make love to him here. Here, anywhere. Any time. 'Will you marry me?' he asked.

CHAPTER TWELVE

HE COULDN'T believe what he'd just said. How had tha happened? Appalled, he sought for a way to turn his mis take into a joke.

But Nicole forestalled him. By saying, 'Yes.' And kiss ing him with such tenderness that he found himself draw ing her gently to the ground, his head a whirl of deligh and panic, though with his body entirely sure of itself.

Nothing seemed real. Not the fever that possessed him the softness of her yielding, eager body, the hasty stripping of their clothes. They melted into one another, the hot curls of sweet agony sending his entire being into spasm as he wicked fingers teased and tormented their way to the seal ing of his fate.

She cried out his name—a raw, feral cry that reache right into his heart. And then, when he could hold back no longer, she whispered in a low moan, 'I love you Blake! I love you so much!'

His mind seemed to shatter into pieces. An emotion rushed in, making him want to shout and cry and punch the air at the same time. Shuddering, he devoured her soft trembling mouth with a tenderness that brought pain to his heart.

He had no idea what was happening to him, only that this must be an explosion of all his long-suppressed feel ings.

Gently he teased apart her thighs. Stroked the silkiness of her. Watched her eyes close in ecstasy as he began those slow, minutely delicate movements that aroused her so sensationally.

She bucked beneath his fingers. Pleaded. Moaned.
Glared and took her own sweet revenge by closing her fist
round where he throbbed with such unbearable heat and
hunger and sliding her hand with exquisite timing until he
thought he'd lose his sanity.

'Love me,' she whispered.

His body obeyed. Every inch was for her, dedicated to
her pleasure. Every word, caress, impassioned glance.

Their bodies were insatiable. He took her with passion,
with gentleness, with laughter. He took her fiercely with
fast, urgent strokes that left them breathless. And then,
after kissing every inch of her skin he made love to her
with a slow deliberation that had them both moaning with
need.

When the sky began to lighten he helped her to dress.
Stumbling together, silent and stunned by what had hap-
pened, they made their way back to the house. Drugged.
Intoxicated. Sated and trembling with emotion.

'Sleep,' he said, when he had seen her to her room.
'Sleep as long as you need, as long as Luc will allow you.
Goodnight.'

He leaned forwards and brushed her lips with his. Stared
deeply into her eyes. Touched her cheek as if he couldn't
believe what they'd done. And slipped quietly away.

Bright-eyed and bursting with happiness, she danced
downstairs in the morning with Luc in her arms. It was
mad and reckless committing yourself to someone you
hardly knew, but she had no doubts about Blake, none at
all.

Her love for him, and his for her, reached deep inside
her, giving her life new meaning. And it would be like that
till she died.

There was a note on the table from Blake, saying he'd
be back for lunch. And so, happily she played with Luc

and then when Mrs Carter arrived she helped by makin
an open French tart until the cook shooed her out for som
fresh air.

'Surely you're not going to hog that baby all to your
self?' Mrs Carter complained, cuddling the squirming Luc
'If you take the path to the wood,' she said craftily, 'yo
might meet Mr Blake on his way back from the farm.'

Nicole laughed. 'There's no fooling you, is there?' sh
murmured.

The cook chuckled. 'I'm not blind. Hurry up, child
Go!'

Nicole kissed her son, nibbled his little bare toes an
waved a cheerful farewell to the approving cook. Livin
here would be wonderful, she thought, her face radian
with happiness.

Being with Blake anywhere would be heaven. Bu
here... She hugged herself with delight, not unaware o
the huge step he'd taken in proposing to her. He must fee
very sure of his love for her, she thought dreamily. It mus
have been as instant and as catastrophically life-changin
as her love was for him.

Marriage. She heaved a huge, happy sigh. Never ha
she been so sure of someone. They were soul-mates. An
she was the happiest woman in the entire world. Dreamin
of their future, she wandered aimlessly through the woo
until she came to a small hut by the path. Intrigued, sh
opened the plank door and stepped inside.

It was then that she heard the thundering of hooves out
side and a man's voice calling in a strange language. Th
hoof beats slowed and stopped.

Cautiously Nicole peered through the glassless window
And felt a shock freeze her where she stood.

Standing beside the fretting Midnight was a man wit
dark hair like Blake's, though it was long and caught a
the nape of the neck with a thin black ribbon. He was olde

and leaner but he had the same presence—and the same piercing eyes the colour of the night sky.

Her heart raced. To her amazement the man was managing to calm the wild, untameable Midnight, whispering into the stallion's ear. And Midnight nuzzled the man's neck and face almost as if he was caressing him.

Intrigued by the man's uncanny resemblance to Blake, she was about to go outside and challenge his right to be here when Midnight suddenly stilled and the man cocked his head in an attitude of listening.

Soon after, Nicole heard the sound of someone running. And she relaxed when she realised it was Blake. But her cry of greeting died on her lips at the sight of Blake's face.

He knew at once. Skidded to a halt, the feeling of shock so fierce that it almost threw him backwards.

His father.

Emotion welled up, depriving him of the ability to speak. For several seconds the two of them just stared at one another, transfixed.

The older man recovered first, lowering his head deferentially. 'Morning, sir,' he said, his voice low and deep. 'This your horse? Fine animal. Got a bit spooked, I reckon. He's all right now.'

'Josef,' Blake said hoarsely, his voice shaking.

There were tears in his eyes. Agonised longing in his heart.

The deference vanished. His father seemed to grow taller, his head held proudly now. And Blake fancied that there was an answering glow of affection and yearning in his father's eyes.

'You know then?' his father said gently.

Blake nodded dumbly. Strode into his father's welcoming arms. A little choke emerged from his throat. His eyes closed and the tears squeezed out.

Both of them were shaking with emotion, muttering and exclaiming their delight. They remained locked together for several long seconds, as if unwilling to part in case this was a dream.

Finally they separated, though keeping their hands on one another's shoulders. Gazing into his father's extraordinary black eyes, he saw the tears that had spiked the dark lashes and trickled down the dark-skinned face.

'Father!' he croaked, choking on a ball of emotion that had lodged in his throat. This was the love he should feel for his father. The love he'd never felt for Darcy. He was overwhelmed with delight. 'You came back!'

'I didn't mean you to see me,' his father said soberly.

'I'm glad I did,' Blake said huskily.

'Me, too. Though it raises problems. Truth is, I've come to see your mother before she dies. Then I will leave her to God and turn away.'

'Why go?' cried Blake, desperate not to lose his father now.

'You know why, son.'

Blake bit his lip. 'I want to get to know you—'

'You will. There'll be time for that. Will she see me do you think?'

He smiled. 'She'll welcome you with open arms. She still loves you,' he said softly.

That evoked a wry, sad smile. 'I thought so. She said I was just a wild fling, but I knew better. You can tell when love hits you. It obliterates everything else.'

'Then…if you knew that, why did you leave her?'

'Because,' Josef said quietly, 'it was what she wanted. And I was prepared to give her everything in my power that she desired. It was the hardest thing I ever did,' he added, 'walking out on the woman I loved and my unborn child.'

Tentatively he touched Blake's chest and his face as if

reassuring himself that this was his son and they had found one another at last. Blake grasped his hand and squeezed it in his. The two men grinned at one another, faintly embarrassed by their intense feelings.

'You're a gypsy,' Blake said, suddenly realising. And understanding of his restless nature flooded through him in a welcome realisation.

'You're not ashamed? Plenty would be,' his father commented drily.

'It's the man I see. Not his label.'

Josef smiled. 'I gave up wandering long ago. Became a craftsman in the village where I live with my mother and my brother and his brood. Always worked for my living. Never dishonest. Never disloyal. True to my family, in the Romany way. You're like me in that. With a touch of wildness and passion. I can see you have the light behind the eyes.'

Blake felt his body ease into itself. 'I feel that I understand myself better,' he said slowly. 'Now I know why I feel so deeply, why I need to feel that I'm free, why I hate routine.'

'Aye. Once we all had wings. Only the gypsies remember how it is to fly,' his father said with a grin.

He thought how apt that was. But he knew someone else who knew how to fly, how to show due wonder at the wonderful world, enjoying every second of life. Little Josef.

'I have a son—you have a grandson named after you. He's very much a free spirit,' Blake said eagerly, longing for his father to meet his namesake.

'I know. I've seen him. Fine lad. And you, Blake, I hear nothing but good, about you.' He grinned at Blake's querying eyebrow. 'I know how to blend into the background. I often sit in the pub with a hat over my head and my collar turned up and listen to the people in the village.

You've done good, here. I'm proud of you. Live. Be
happy. You only come this way once.'

'I know!' Blake replied fervently. 'My mother says the
same. I mean to be what I am—and to go for what I want.'

Frozen to the spot and with all the colour drained from
her horrified face, Nicole watched Blake and his true father
embrace again.

What he wanted. What did he mean? Her heart thudded
painfully.

'My existence was supposed to be a secret,' Blake's
father reproached.

'It was, until a short time ago. But, because she is dying,
she wanted to unburden herself,' she heard Blake say. 'At
first I could hardly believe I wasn't Darcy's son. And then
she showed me the picture of you she carries and I knew
it to be true. I suppose I'd *felt* it to be true all my life.'

Josef looked delighted. 'My picture,' he said softly.
'Well, well. Take me to her. And don't worry. No one will
see me, I'll make sure of that. The resemblance between
us is so strong that it would be obvious you're not Darcy's
spawn. And you don't want anyone to find out you're not
the heir, do you?'

She didn't hear Blake's quiet reply. There was a roaring
in her ears like thunder. Now it had been said. Not the
heir. *Not the heir!*

That man was Blake's father! Not Darcy Bellamie, but
another man who had loved Blake's mother and got her
with child, whom she had pretended was the heir to
Cranford!

Dizziness attacked her and she almost lost her balance.
But the terror of being discovered helped her to steady
herself. Trying to control her violent shaking and fighting
to stay quiet when she wanted to scream questions at
Blake, she became aware that the two men were moving

away, talking too quietly for her to hear, with the devoted Midnight trotting submissively behind them.

When it was safe to do so she collapsed weakly against the window, gripping the glazing bar for dear life.

It was then that the nightmare began. Horror flooded through her. If Blake wasn't the heir at all…then she was. That meant… The implication hit her like a blow to the stomach. Blake knew very well that he had no right to Cranford. But, by marrying her, he would be the husband of the true heir.

Her fist went to her mouth to stop the primal wail that fought to emerge and she bit into the flesh, tasting it.

Surely, she thought, he hadn't been covering his back by proposing to her? But it all made a horrible kind of sense. She forced herself to think.

There had been Blake's initial hostility when he knew who she was. His lies about her father and his determination to send her home, then his change of tack when she'd insisted on staying. And finally he'd shown a personal interest in her…

She felt sick. Perhaps everything had been a sham! Blake had been so scared of losing his position that he'd…he'd…

'No. *No!*' she moaned.

He couldn't have faked that raw hunger. Nor the love in his eyes, surely? Was it a coincidence that they'd fallen in love? Or…had it been a calculated act to secure the Bellamie inheritance for ever? She shivered, feeling chilled to the bone.

Questions piled up in her head so thick and fast that she put her hands to her ears to block her senses. Her stomach lurched and she ran out and was sick.

With distaste she cleaned herself up. Now she had to face him. But what would she do, what would she say? Denounce him as a liar and an impostor?

If she did, then she'd pull the wrath of the village about her ears and she and Luc wouldn't be able to manage Cranford. And if his mother knew that her deception had been discovered then maybe that might hasten her death.

But this land was hers! Eventually it would be Luc's! She couldn't let Blake get away with this scam. He didn't deserve to. Yet…what would she do as mistress of Cranford, alone in that great house with her baby?

Confused and miserable, she stood there in the beautiful woodland, recognising it was rightfully hers and yet knowing she was incapable of claiming it. She couldn't run the estate, even with the goodwill of everyone behind her. The thought of managing such a huge enterprise without any experience at all was terrifying.

Besides, she wanted Blake. Wanted to pretend that everything was fine and that he loved her for herself alone, not because she had Bellamie blood. She acknowledged that the marriage might be one-sided. She'd be unloved, eventually rejected. Would it be worth that humiliation to be with the man she loved so stupidly, so obsessively that her brain had gone into hibernation? She didn't know. Couldn't decide.

Pale and trembling, she slowly began the walk back, turning everything over in her mind. Perhaps he did truly love her.

A nasty little voice queried cynically, After such a short time? But she pushed it away. She had to believe in Blake. To do otherwise would destroy her.

'Well! Your walk didn't do you much good!' exclaimed Mrs Carter when Nicole shuffled disconsolately in through the back door. Wan-faced, she immediately went to Luc and hugged his warm, loving little body to her for reassurance.

'I have a terrible headache,' she mumbled, preparing to feed her son and hoping she'd be forgiven the lie this once.

This was her future. Loving Luc. Protecting him and ensuring that he learnt how to run Cranford. But, her conscience nagged her, what of little Josef? She put her hand to her throat as she gagged.

'Nicole!'

At Blake's voice—kind, concerned and deceptively loving—she closed her eyes, fighting the nausea and concentrating on Luc. The tug at her breast. Her child. Her flesh and blood. He'd never betray her. He was all she could rely on for undying, uncomplicated love.

'Sweetheart!'

There was a rustle as he crouched down in front of her. The familiar electric charge making the air between them tremble. His hands steadied her arms and a false sense of calm and security soothed her.

'Just a sick headache,' she forced out. And suddenly it became real, hitting her with such splitting ferocity that she moaned aloud.

His gentle fingers stroked her forehead. 'What can I do?' he asked tenderly.

Love me! she wanted to cry. Tell me that you don't care that I am your means of keeping Cranford, that you feel as passionately for me as I do for you!

'A nice cup of tea. What do you think?' came the kindly tones of Mrs Carter.

She'd throw up. Her head shook imperceptibly.

'No, thanks,' she whispered. 'I want to be alone. In the dark.'

Her head was being stroked again, the finger-light movements so delicate and caring that she could almost pretend he loved her.

'I can't bear to see you like this,' he said softly.

No, she thought bitterly. Until we're married your future isn't certain! You'll look after me like a gardener caring for his prize marrow! And then... She gritted her teeth.

Once they were married her purpose would have been served. Her head tipped back in despair.

'I'll take Luc when you've finished—' he began.

'No!' Her eyes opened, wild and frantic. He wasn't going to have her child! She blinked, seeing Mrs Carter's open-mouthed astonishment. Sensed Blake's surprise in the cessation of his soothing fingers. 'I want him with me,' she whispered. 'He'll be ready for his sleep, anyway.'

When Luc had finished feeding and she had winded and changed him, Blake helped her up the stairs. The touch of his hands and the close hug of his body was driving her to distraction. He was living a lie! she told herself miserably.

But hope and love made her wonder if that was true, and if perhaps he did really adore her. Because, she thought with a scowl, he was giving a darn good impression of loving concern!

He drew the curtains, bringing coolness and darkness to the room.

'Do you want me to stay?' he murmured when he had coaxed her into stripping down to her underwear and sliding into bed.

'Hold my hand!' she muttered before she could stop herself.

He clasped it firmly, for all the world as if he was willing her to get better because she was one of the most important people in his life. Which she was, of course, the nasty little voice said. She was bringing him the inheritance he coveted.

'What…?' She licked her dry mouth. The question had to be asked. She must know her position. 'What would have happened,' she said weakly, 'if you had been a girl?'

'I would have worn dresses,' he murmured, amused.

Her brow furrowed in irritation. There was no time for humour. 'I mean to Cranford.'

His hand brushed the hair from her forehead and she noticed that his fingers were shaking slightly. Then his mouth touched the deep frown line between her brows.

'Your father would have inherited,' he said in an odd, husky tone.

'So...it goes through the male line.'

'Yes, darling. But why bother your head with that now?' he asked, a slight tension underlying his words.

'Why indeed.'

For the first time in her life she was keeping something back. Now she knew that Luc was the heir she felt frightened for her son. Terrible, uncharitable thoughts were streaming unchecked through her mind. Fiercely, she tried to reassure herself. Blake wouldn't hurt Luc. He was a good man.

And yet he was keeping Luc's inheritance a secret. Was marrying her as a safeguard.

'My darling,' he murmured. 'Are you daunted by the thought of becoming my wife and mistress of Cranford?'

Her eyes filled with tears as she gazed into his glowing eyes. 'Yes,' she said honestly, in a small, pinched voice.

'You'll be fine. I'll guide you,' he murmured, kissing her cheek tenderly.

'Blake...' She searched his face for the truth. 'You...do love me, don't you?'

He smiled as if she were being silly. 'You are the most wonderful thing that's happened to me—apart from Josef's birth,' he assured her.

She closed her eyes, trying hard to regulate her breathing, because that wasn't what she'd wanted to hear at all. Her suspicious mind was telling her that she might be the most wonderful thing that had happened. But not because Blake had fallen in love with her.

She put her hand to her aching head. He'd been in danger before she'd arrived. Someone might have learnt the

secret of his birth. But as her husband he could rest easy.
Till he grew tired of being polite and pretending, and abandoned her.

'I'll leave you.'

Her eyes snapped open in instant fear. 'What?'

'Just for a short time. Let you sleep it off.' He gave her
a quick peck on the cheek. 'I'll get on with the arrange-
ments for the wedding. I hope you're in as big a hurry as
I am!'

He flashed his dazzling grin, blew her a kiss and walked
softly out.

Nicole stared up at the ceiling. A hasty courtship, an
even hastier marriage! How suspicious was that?

'Oh, please let him love me!' she moaned.

But she had no idea how she'd ever know—until it was
too late. Or how she could salve her conscience where
Josef was concerned. The child expected to inherit. If she
said nothing, then he would. If she stuck up for Luc and
for what was right, then little Josef would be utterly devastated.

It was a terrible situation. And she had no idea what to
do.

CHAPTER THIRTEEN

SHE refused lunch. In the semi-darkened room she stared up at the ceiling, her mind a merciful blank because her headache was so bad she couldn't think about her situation any more.

Blake crept in and she closed her eyes, hoping he'd go away, but he sat by the bed. She couldn't stand being watched any longer. What was he doing? she thought irritably. Guarding his meal-ticket?

Her eyes opened. He looked so anxious and loving that her heart turned over. His lips lightly touched hers.

'Anything I can get you?' he whispered.

The truth! she wanted to scream. Instead, she weakly muttered that she'd be better on her own. And then decided to test him. It sickened her that she was playing a game and not confronting him, but she wanted to give him a chance to confess.

'I was in the wood earlier,' she mumbled.

He flinched visibly and it was a while before he answered. 'Nice walk?'

'I thought,' she whispered faintly, 'I saw you. With someone.'

The silence was so thick it seemed to close around her like a blanket.

'A man who used to know my mother,' Blake replied.

She waited. But he said no more.

'A visitor to see her?' she asked, the misery filling every cell in her body. 'She only lets you and little Josef into her sick room. She hasn't even met me.'

'This man was a special friend.'

Nicole tried to sound amused. 'An old lover?' she asked with a raised eyebrow. Please tell me, she begged with her eyes. Tell me.

Blake shrugged. 'I must go. You'll be all right?'

And he had kissed her, his lips cold and his eyes distant, and had reached the door before she could say anything more.

She closed her eyes tightly. He needed time. He'd had a shock when his father had turned up and would need to think things through.

'Fine. I'll sleep.' She even managed a weak smile. 'See you later.'

With a look of relief, he hurried out as if he had been released from jail.

Nicole lay there trembling. When he'd had time to consider his options he'd realise what he must do, she told herself. It was wonderful that he had met his father. It had been an emotional moment for both of them.

And a devastating one for her.

The afternoon dragged. Eventually she slept. Refused supper. Allowed herself to be coaxed with a small bowl of soup and nodded when Blake told her that Josef was anxious to see her.

On the tip of her tongue was the question, Which Josef? But she didn't ask it and raised herself against the pillows when the little boy tiptoed in, heartbreakingly the image of his father and grandfather.

'Are you any better?' Josef asked in a loud stage whisper.

'I am a little. And will be fine in the morning,' she said, thinking how much she loved this child. Her eyes filled with tears and Blake, seeing this, took her hand in his.

'I brought you something I made in school today,' Josef hissed, taking huge, exaggeratedly soft steps on his way to her bedside.

Her heart melted. 'Did you?' she said fondly.

He thrust a strange concoction at her—a painted cereal box with precarious additions. Conscious of the honour he was bestowing on her, she received it gravely.

'I dropped it on the way back,' he explained, tugging at a drunken piece of an egg box. 'We were playing football and it sort of ended up in the bushes with the ball. Do you like it?'

She recognised the wisteria that had been painted over the neatly scissored front door. 'Cranford.' she smiled. 'Thank you.' And said from the bottom of her heart, 'I will treasure it always.'

Josef beamed at her and his father. 'She would make a lovely Mummy, Dad,' he said wistfully.

Blake drew in a breath. Smiled at her. And she froze. But it was too late. 'I think so too,' he said.

Josef's eyes widened. 'You mean…?'

His father laughed. 'I mean.'

'Wow—oh!' Josef clapped a hand to his mouth to stem his exuberant yell. 'Wow!' he whispered. 'Oh, wow, wow, wow!' he squealed as quietly as his joy would allow. 'Are you going to be married?'

'As soon as possible,' Blake replied.

The look he gave her was one of pure love. And she responded, smiling with blind happiness, because her brain just wasn't connected to her heart at all.

'And you'll be my Mummy?' Josef snuggled up to Nicole.

She tucked her arm around him, praying that everything would be all right.

'You have a mother. I will be like a mother,' she said gently.

'Make cakes with chocolate drops on and gooey icing?'

'Yes,' she replied, breaking her heart with love for Blake and his motherless son.

'And we'll have picnics and you'll tell me off when I fall in the river and things?' he said earnestly.

'Definitely.'

'I'm so happy,' Josef sighed. 'I can teach Luc how to ride. And how to catch fish. And he can be my brother and share *everything* with me!'

She felt Blake stiffen. 'I think we should leave Nicole to rest now,' he said, clearing his throat.

Gently Josef wound his arms around her neck and kissed her on both cheeks. 'Goodnight,' he said with such infinite tenderness and love that it stopped her heart for a moment and she couldn't breathe for the pain that ripped through her. 'Oh, Daddy, isn't it wonderful?' he cried. 'I want to go out and shout for a bit before I go to bed, if that's all right. I've got all these yells and ''wow''s bottled up inside me and they've got to be let out or I'll bust.'

'Sure!' chuckled Blake. 'I know how you feel.' He sobered. 'I have the same feelings.' His voice shook. 'It's how we are, Josef.'

With a loving kiss, he left her too and she heard Josef's excited chatter echoing down the corridor and then his erupting delight as he let rip once he thought he was out of earshot.

Blake loved her, she told herself. Didn't he?

Then she remembered how he'd said what Josef meant to him. She knew that sense of protection too and understood that he might do anything for his son. Even marry a woman he didn't love.

The bones of her spine seemed to turn to ice. Blake had deceived her. Deceived everyone. He and his mother had lived a lie for their own ends—and they'd said terrible things about her father.

That hurt so much that she was beyond crying. In the white heat of pain she recognised that Blake would keep his secret for his son's sake. And the lie would fester between them like a sore until it became an open wound.

He slipped into bed with her later. Held her very gently as if she were precious china. And she lay awake when he slept, adoring him and torn between staying silent for ever and confessing that she knew the truth.

She grew cold in his arms and that must have woken him.

'Headache worse?' he murmured drowsily. 'I could get you something for it—'

'No,' she whispered. 'It's gone. Hold me, Blake. Hold me!'

Surprised by her passion, he wrapped her in his arms, kissing her face tenderly. 'Headache!' he said in mock reproof. 'And we're not even married!'

She managed a little laugh but couldn't speak because her distress filled every cavity of her body.

'Have you...loved before?' she asked shakily.

'No. I haven't even dated since my marriage broke up.' She waited for him to say the words she longed to hear. But waited in vain.

'We must tell Mother. Introduce you.' His mouth drifted over her cheekbone and down her jaw. 'Josef is thrilled. I could hardly get him into bed. I'm afraid he has a long list of what mummies and daddies do. One of which is to share a bath.'

She did smile then. 'I'm glad he's pleased. He's very important to you, isn't he?'

'Yes.' Blake's voice was husky. 'I want to protect him from hurt. The trouble is, I know that's impossible,' he muttered. 'He will be hurt. It's inevitable.' The bleakness of his face caused a pain to slice through her. He was finding this situation impossible too, she realised. The suffering radiated from him in waves and she wanted to take that suffering away.

Nicole couldn't bear to see him like this. And suddenly she knew what she must do. Loving him as she did, finding his pain worse than her own, she had to make the sacrifice.

'Make love to me,' she whispered, suddenly frantic to be as close, as intimate with him as possible.

They both seemed to need one another with the same desperation. They tore at one another's clothes. He was hot and hard and urgent and she didn't care if he felt just lust or if it was love because she felt impelled to give him everything—her heart, her soul, her mind and body. This was how she felt. How much she loved him. And she would give him all she could and he would know that her love had been unfaltering.

The night was a magical one. It seemed that he worshipped her and she allowed herself to believe this.

She could keep silent because she loved Blake so much. Because she felt the same about Josef. And because she knew Joe would look after Luc's future. That was her decision.

She moaned beneath Blake's fierce loving. Urged him on, writhing and arching her body, taunting him and luring him until he groaned with frustration.

And then they slid together, united, each shuddering with pleasure. Slowly, with agonising tension, they moved in perfect rhythm, watching one another, drowning in each other's eyes until she saw Blake's head go back and heard his breath shorten, felt his heart accelerate and then lost herself in the exquisite pleasure of their mutual climax.

'I love you,' she whispered as he kissed her passionately afterwards.

'Oh, Nicole!' he rasped, and buried his face in her neck.

She clenched her jaw. No word of love. And that was what she must accept, even if it broke her heart in the process.

* * *

She woke early the next morning and Blake had already gone. She fancied she'd heard the clatter of hooves on the cobbles in the stable yard. She smiled at that, realising he would be riding off his tension and guilt. There would be many fast gallops in the future, she imagined. And wondered what she would do to keep her own sanity.

After feeding Luc and making herself breakfast, she decided to go for a walk to blow away the cobwebs and to come to terms with her decision to say nothing.

Pushing the buggy and with her head down as she frowned and thought, she didn't realise until too late that she was heading straight for Blake, who was standing by the lakeside with Midnight and watching her approach. She stopped, disconcerted. Her heart thumped as usual because he looked so handsome. Her body came instantly to life and she wanted to run to him and fling herself into his arms.

But he seemed detached and distant, his brooding eyes dark and his brows meeting in a fierce scowl. Nicole gulped, suddenly apprehensive and a chill settled on her body.

'What is it?' The wind tossed her hair as she remained a few feet away. His manner wasn't welcoming.

Pain wrenched across his face. 'I must talk to you,' he growled.

Instantly she felt afraid. If he was going to confess then she didn't want to know. It would end their relationship because he'd leave—

'Nicole,' he said curtly. 'Come and sit down. You must listen to me.'

'No!' Petrified of the consequences she backed away. 'I—I have to go back—'

He let go of Midnight's reins and strode towards her, grim and stony-faced. His hands caught her arms and he reached out a foot to toe the brake on the buggy, then pulled her to the ground without ceremony or gentleness.

'No,' she protested, struggling to free herself from her tangle of long skirts. 'I don't want to listen—'

'You must!' he said hoarsely, holding her down. 'It has to be said. It's about your father.'

Surprised, she stopped fighting him. 'My father?'

'I spoke to Mother about him,' he said quickly. 'She has admitted that she lied about his behaviour. She doesn't know why he left. He just disappeared overnight. But all my enquiries confirm that he was a good man, Nicole. A brilliant artist. Everyone was fond of him and you were right. I apologise. I was mistaken to believe her. Please forgive me.'

'Of course,' she said mechanically. 'I understand why you believed her and not me.'

'Forgive her too, if you can. She was only trying to protect me. All her life she has put my interests first. She deeply regrets maligning him. Don't you want to know why she lied?'

'No!' she whispered. Desperate to finish the conversation, she made to get up and was prevented.

'You must be curious why she blackened your father's name!' he grated harshly, his face contorted with misery.

She could see how painful this was for him. She flung him a reassuring smile and wished she could escape his imprisoning grasp. Make a quip. Pretend everything was fine.

'Not at all,' she began lightly.

'Listen, Nicole!' he growled, forcing up her chin so that she had to look at him. 'This is something that will change your life—'

'I don't want it changed!' she blurted out wildly, scared now he was close to confessing. 'I just want you! To love

you, to be your wife! Nothing else, Blake! Do you understand? I want nothing else!'

She saw the anguish ripping through him, felt the con-
traction of his muscles as he steeled himself to deny the
inheritance and to ruin his son's future. So she kissed him.
Hotly. Passionately, tasting his mouth, driving him to the
ground.

Until he rolled away impatiently, his face like thunder.
They stared at one another for a moment, his chest heaving, her breasts straining at her shirt. And she knew with
a terrible sinking feeling in her stomach that he would not
be stopped.

'The truth is inescapable. She wanted me to think badly
of your father because she thought he was still alive. In
her pain and misery she blurted out the first things that
came into her head. She didn't want the risk that I might
contact him. You see... I am not the rightful heir to
Cranford,' he said in a hoarse whisper.

She closed her eyes. He had chosen to do what was
morally right. And his action had broken him.

'Nicole?'

He could see by her anguished face that the truth was
hitting her. Soon she would wonder if he'd proposed to
her as a means of keeping Cranford in his grasp.

'No,' she moaned, shaking her head.

She sat there, a tight ball of tension, her lip quivering
and misery in every line of her face. She would see this
as a betrayal and nothing he could say would ever make
her trust him again.

Never in his entire life had he felt so desolate. Not only
would he lose Cranford, but Nicole as well. But he
couldn't cheat her of what was her son's right to own the
estate.

A frustrated fury burst from him. 'I have to tell you! I
can't keep it a secret any longer! My mother had a lover.

I am the child of that lover. Therefore I am a *bastard*! That man you saw was my real father.'

She bit her lip. He knew what she was thinking so when she said it he wasn't surprised. 'Is that why you're telling me?' she asked in a small voice. 'Because he's turned up and therefore you were about to be exposed as an impostor?'

'No. He said he'd keep a low profile. But I don't want him to hide! I'm not ashamed of him! I wanted it all: Cranford, you, him. And now I know that's impossible. I had decided to tell you before we were married—even before he arrived. I was waiting for the right moment. So there it is. I have no Bellamie blood. The inheritance cannot pass down my line. That leaves you as the nearest next of kin. It means that Luc is the heir.'

He paused, waiting for her to speak. She seemed to be in shock and no wonder. He swallowed, taking the final step, the words lurching out hoarsely as emotion claimed him and he spelt out her fears for her.

'I know you will think that I wanted to marry you because it would allow me to stay here—'

'Did that ever cross your mind?' she whispered, looking terrified.

He couldn't spare her. He'd told himself that she would get the truth, nothing less.

'When I first knew who you were, and when I realised there was a sexual attraction between us,' he replied with a sense of scouring shame, 'I thought you might be willing to live with me, to share the benefits of the estate—'

'Not…marriage.'

God. This sounded so bad. 'Not then.'

'What changed your mind? Why did you propose?' she asked mournfully.

Her eyes haunted him. For the rest of his life he woul

remember their reproach. 'I don't know,' he admitted in a harsh whisper. 'It—it just came out.'

'Not very flattering,' she said jerkily.

He pushed his hand through his hair. 'I'm trying to be honest here. The proposal surprised me. I've no idea where it came from. Somewhere inside me. My soul... Hell!' he groaned. 'You must hate me and I wouldn't blame you for that. I'll go as soon as I can. Leave the estate to your care.' He swallowed, unable to bear the prospect. 'I just need time to tell my mother and Josef and to organise somewhere for them to stay. And to say goodbye to everyone.'

Nicole felt as if her heart was tearing in two. He turned his head away but the broken, haunted look on his face stayed with her. It had come from his soul, she thought. What did he mean by that?

'Say something!' he whispered. 'For God's sake, say something!'

'You can't do this to Josef,' she said shakily.

The strong jaw clenched. 'I have to. He will understand.'

From his soul...

Her head lifted. She couldn't put Blake and Josef through this. She'd never live with herself. She would gladly sacrifice everything for his happiness.

'He won't need to.'

Blake frowned. Turned to look at her. 'What?'

Now that the truth was out in the open she couldn't stay if he really didn't care for her. She would leave the coast clear for him.

However...if he *did* care—as she believed he did in her heart of hearts—then he could have everything he desired.

Her body grew erect. Her future happiness hung on a knife edge.

From his soul. Let that be true!

'I'm going back to France,' she announced, taking the gamble. His brow furrowed and she made it clearer. 'Blood isn't important. It's the man,' she said, partly echoing something Blake had said to his father. 'And you and Josef will run Cranford better than I could. Luc doesn't know anything of this and will be none the wiser. Keep Cranford. You've given it your love and tender care all these years and you deserve it.'

He just stared at her. For several seconds it seemed he was trying to make sense of what she'd said. 'You…you would give up a life of luxury and wealth…for my benefit?' he eventually asked in a cracked voice.

She smiled. 'Of course. I love you more than I can say,' she told him simply. 'I want what makes you happy.'

'But I wouldn't be! How can I ever be happy?' he raged.

It was her turn to stare. Her pulses began to race. 'Why's that?' she asked with as much innocence as she could. 'You would have Cranford. Josef. What more do you need?'

Blake scowled at the ground. Fixed her with his penetrating glare. '*You*! You wouldn't be with me!' he growled.

'No,' she said, hardly able to conceal her delight. 'No if I'm in France.'

'Then I'll follow you there!' he cried grimly, capturing her in his arms. 'I'll prove I love you if I have to set up home next to you and court you for the next ten years!' he cried passionately. 'I *have* to be with you, Nicole. Life is unthinkable without you. I knew that some time ago and the intensity of my feelings scared the hell out of me! probably loved you from the moment I first saw you, but I was too dim to realise it. If you want my happiness, then that includes you. If you love me be my wife. I want nothing less. I know you can't trust me and I'll wait for as long as it takes for you to realise what I truly feel. I was *you.* Selfishly, for myself. For Josef too. I want us to be a family. To have picnics together—'

'Take baths together,' she suggested in delight, a wicked look in her eyes.

He pushed her back and scanned her amused face. 'Let me follow you!' he groaned. 'I love you, Nicole! So much that it hurts as if I'm being knifed! I can think of nothing else but you. Want to be with you all the time, touching you, looking at you…'

His mouth closed on hers, possessive and demanding. She wound her arms around his neck and surrendered to his kiss.

'It seems a shame to go all the way to France,' she murmured in his ear some time later.

'Nicole? My darling?' he whispered, hope making his voice shake.

Her mouth found his. 'I believe that you do love me. We were both shot by the same arrow, I think. It pierced both our hearts very early on.'

'The moment I set eyes on you,' he agreed.

She smiled. 'So we might as well stay here, don't you think? The boys can share Cranford. And any other children we might have can share it too.'

'Other…children?' he croaked.

'Mm. Am I being forward? Brazen?'

He grinned and their lips met in a long, lingering kiss. 'Oh, I do hope so,' he murmured. 'Do you mind if I let off steam somehow? I have all this energy inside me waiting for me to shout and yell and go ''wow''!'

'We could combine the two,' she suggested, looking deceptively demure. 'Link up our plan to have more children and you letting off some of that energy.'

'Good idea,' he breathed, drawing her to her feet.

But they stood there for a very long time, just kissing tenderly, holding one another.

And, gazing into his rapturous face, Nicole felt such a profound love for him that, for a while, just being with him was enough.

'I love you so much!' he murmured dazedly.

And she lost herself in the gentle wonder of his kiss.

'It's getting dark. Draw the curtains back a little more and let the last of the daylight in, my darling Josef,' wheezed Kay Bellamie.

It wasn't dark at all. The light streamed in but Josef knew that, for her, the light was fading.

He made a pretence of dragging the drapes back and stood at the open window, watching his son and Giles's daughter stand up and embrace lovingly where before they seemed to have been locked in some kind of stand-off.

'I hope Blake understands why I lied about Giles. I feel so bad about it. I've been selfish and wrong,' Kay fretted. 'And his pride and honour will ensure that he loses Cranford—'

'No. By some miracle it is securely his,' Josef said gently.

She had to know. He sat beside her and told her how the young Giles had secretly fallen in love with a village girl who'd died tragically when she'd been working on Cranford farm. Josef explained how he'd made some silver bracelets for the girl who'd died before Giles could give them to her. How the distraught young man had been unable to bear the sight of Cranford after that and had fled the unhappy memories.

'After that he would only have given those bracelets to someone he loved deeply,' he murmured. 'To his daughter. The girl who came to scatter her father's ashes around the churchyard, the girl who is so like her father that it touched my heart when I saw her. The woman Blake has fallen in love with. The pattern of life has come full circle and completed itself. They will be happy together, you can be sure of that.'

He saw the silent tears and hoped he hadn't given her too great a shock. 'Kay,' he said tenderly, stroking her hand in his. 'Are you happy at last?'

She smiled at him, the old, dazzling smile, her eyes the colour of the summer sky. 'I am. Thank you for telling me. For being here,' she said faintly. 'I am very, very happy. I love you, Josef. And always will.'

'And I have always loved you, Kay. No other woman. Just you.'

He choked back his own tears and kissed her tenderly on the lips. As he did so he felt her relax and her life ebbed away in a soft whisper.

Looking down on her, he didn't see a woman old before her time because of severe pain but the beautiful girl with whom he had fallen head over heels in love.

'We'll meet again,' he said softly.

Raising his head, he saw through the blur of tears that Blake and Nicole were walking hand in hand back to the house. He would tell them later about Kay. How content she'd been. That her love had burned, like his, down the years and eventually she'd been at peace with herself.

And then into his vision came a Common Blue butterfly, the colour of the sky. It fluttered into the room, beating its wings frantically against the window. The old Romany legend had come true for him.

Gently, reverently, he cupped his hand around the fragile butterfly. And, with love filling his heart, he set it free.

Modern Romance™
...seduction and
passion guaranteed

Tender Romance™
...love affairs that
last a lifetime

Medical Romance™
...medical drama
on the pulse

Historical Romance™
...rich, vivid and
passionate

Sensual Romance™
...sassy, sexy and
seductive

Blaze Romance™
...the temperature's
rising

27 new titles every month.

Live the emotion

MILLS & BOON®

M

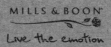

MILLS & BOON

Live the emotion

Modern Romance™

HIS BOARDROOM MISTRESS *by Emma Darcy*

Liz Hart is the ultimate PA – highly efficient and almost invisible to her boss. But her sisters persuade her to have a make-over with devastating results! Cole Pierson is curious to see a stranger at his secretary's desk – and stunned to realise it's Liz!

THE BLACKMAIL MARRIAGE *by Penny Jordan*

Prince Luc D'Urbino needs a wife to solve the turmoil in his Mediterranean principality. Years ago, Carrie Broadbent shared a night of passion with Luc – she is more than a little surprised now, when he returns and demands they marry…

THEIR SECRET BABY *by Kate Walker*

Caitlin has heard nothing good about her cousin's husband, Rhys Morgan. So when Amelie makes Caitlin guardian to her baby by another man, she sees no reason to contact him. But irresistible Rhys believes that baby Fleur is *his* daughter, and he'll do anything to get her back…

HIS CINDERELLA MISTRESS *by Carole Mortimer*

January Calendar is too busy helping her sisters to spend time waiting for Prince Charming! Millionaire lawyer Max Golding thinks January is too cold – towards him! He's determined to bring about a thaw – and how better to do it than melt her heart in the warmth of his bed?

On sale 2nd January 2004

Available at most branches of WHSmith, Tesco, Martins, Borders, Eason, Sainsbury's and all good paperback bookshops.

1203/01a

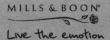

FREE

4 BOOKS
AND A SURPRISE GIFT!

We would like to take this opportunity to thank you for reading this Mills & Boon® book b
offering you the chance to take FOUR more specially selected titles from the Modern Romance
series absolutely FREE! We're also making this offer to introduce you to the benefits
the Reader Service™ —

- ★ FREE home delivery
- ★ FREE monthly Newsletter
- ★ FREE gifts and competitions
- ★ Exclusive Reader Service discount
- ★ Books available before they're in the shops

Accepting these FREE books and gift places you under no obligation to buy; you may canc
at any time, even after receiving your free shipment. Simply complete your details below ar
return the entire page to the address below. **You don't even need a stamp!**

YES! Please send me 4 free Modern Romance™ books and a surprise gift. I understand th
unless you hear from me, I will receive 6 superb new titles every month for just £2.0
each, postage and packing free. I am under no obligation to purchase any books and may can
my subscription at any time. The free books and gift will be mine to keep in any case.

P3ZEI

Ms/Mrs/Miss/Mr ....Initials ....
BLOCK CAPITALS PLE
Surname ....
Address ....
....
....Postcode ....

Send this whole page to:
UK: FREEPOST CN81, Croydon, CR9 3WZ
EIRE: PO Box 4546, Kilcock, County Kildare (stamp required)